Greenleaf S. Tukey, Walter E. Simmons

Our Country's Defenders

A Military Drama in Five Acts

Greenleaf S. Tukey, Walter E. Simmons

Our Country's Defenders
A Military Drama in Five Acts

ISBN/EAN: 9783337376413

Printed in Europe, USA, Canada, Australia, Japan

Cover: Foto ©Andreas Hilbeck / pixelio.de

More available books at **www.hansebooks.com**

Our Country's Defenders!

A MILITARY DRAMA IN FIVE ACTS.

WRITTEN BY

GREENLEAF S. TUKEY, WALTER E. SIMMONS,
PHILIPP W. GOLLIFF.

———○○⦂❀⦂○○———

BOSTON:
ROCKWELL & CHURCHILL, PRINTERS,
122 WASHINGTON STREET.
1873.

TO

JOSEPH HOOKER POST 23, DEPARTMENT OF MASS.,

G. A. R.

THIS PLAY IS RESPECTFULLY DEDICATED BY THE

AUTHORS.

Any persons playing this piece without the consent of the authors will be prosecuted to the utmost extent of the law.

All communications should be addressed to

PHILIPP W. GOLLIFF, Business Agent,

191 WEBSTER STREET,

East Boston, Mass.

CAST OF CHARACTERS,

AS ORIGINALLY PERFORMED BY

JOSEPH HOOKER POST 23, G. A. R.,

East Boston, April 22, 1872.

Edward Clifford .	.	Greenleaf S. Tukey
Guy Lockwood .	.	Walter E. Simmons
Sam'l Huntington	.	Geo. A. Butler
Charles Huntington } *his sons*	.	Wm. A. Waterhouse
Harry Huntington }	.	W. S. Greenough
Wm. Bryant	.	Geo. E. Harrington
Alphonse DePeyster .	.	Wm. A. McLarty
Nath'l Foster	.	Isaac B. Noble
Fritz Speigelhalter	.	John Henry
Tom Swift .	.	Samuel Holt
Capt. Gregg	.	W. H. Warner
Pompey	.	Geo. H. Rymill
Policeman .	.	Geo. H. Brown
Capt. Perry }	.	A. N. Proctor
Lieut. Harrison } *of the*	.	S. P. Hampton
Tom Marlinspike } *ship Pembroke* .	.	H. A. Lampher
Jack Tarbox }	.	S. S. Sampson
Pedlar .	.	Charles Melville
Dr. Swett .	.	J. C. Littlefield
Jas. Harris } *Union*	.	F. V. Christian
Henry Crittenden } *Privates* .	.	Frank E. Dodge
Newsboy .	.	Master Wm. McBride
Major McKee }	.	Wm. H. Lewis
Capt. Toombs } *Confederates* .	.	Geo. H. Whalebone
Wm. Small }	.	Edw. Smith
Maud Huntington	.	Mrs. Georgie C. Metcalf
Lucy Clifton .	.	Miss Mary Kezer
Widow DePeyster .	.	Mrs. Wm. H. Lawrence

Nurses, Goddess of Liberty, angel, soldiers, sailors, citizens, etc.

COSTUMES.

Samuel Huntington. Modern suit of black, gray wig and side whiskers.

Cha's Huntington. First — Modern suit. Second — Union Colonel's full dress.

Harry Huntington. First — Modern suit. Second — Union Sergeant. Third — old rags. Fourth — dressing-gown and slippers.

Edw. Clifford. First — Modern suit. Second — Union Sergeant. Third — old rags. Fourth — shirt sleeves.

Guy Lockwood. First — Modern suit. Second — Rebel Colonel Cavalry uniform.

Wm. Bryant. First — Modern suit. Second — Union Corporal. Third — old rags.

Alphonse DePeyster. First — Modern suit. Second — Union Private. Third — old rags.

Nath'l Foster. First — Modern suit. Second — Union Sergeant. Third — old rags. Iron-gray wig and whiskers.

Fritz Speigelhalter. First — Dutch suit. Second — Union Private.

Thomas Swift. First — Modern suit. Second — Union Private. Third — old rags. (This character is intended to be made up fat, until the Prison Scene.)

Capt. Gregg. Union Captain's uniform.

Pompey. Full Contraband costume.

Dr. Swett. First — Union Lieutenant's suit. Second — Modern suit.

Capt. Perry. Naval Captain's uniform. Gray wig and whiskers.

Lieut. Harrison. Undress Navy uniform.

Jack Tarbox
Tom Marlingspike } Union sailors' costume.

Maud Huntington. First — Modern evening suit. Second — plain black suit.

Lucy Clifton. Plain black suit.

Widow DePeyster. Plain black suit.

Nurses. Black dresses.

Wigs and beards for stockade scene.

Goddess of Liberty, angel, soldiers, citizens, etc., in appropriate costumes, according to their respective characters.

TIME — 1861.

Time of performance two hours forty-five minutes.

OUR COUNTRY'S DEFENDERS.

ACT I.

SCENE I. — HUNTINGTON's *private office.* — *Enter* NATHANIEL, R., *with books and papers; sets them down, and arranges office.*

Nath'l. Quarter to nine, and none of the boys here yet. It's all very well for them as long as the old man comes late, but some fine day he will take it into his head to come early, and then look out, Mr. Billy. (*Noise in outer office.*) There they are, and just in time, too, for here comes Huntington.

Enter HUNTINGTON, R.

Hunt. Good morning, Nathaniel.
Nath'l. Good morning, sir.

(HUNTINGTON *takes coat off, sits, looks over papers and mail.*)

Hunt. Where's Edward?
Nath'l. He has just stepped out a moment, sir. He will be in directly.

(HUNTINGTON *lays down paper, and remarks:*)

Hunt. What a mixed-up state of affairs the country is in at present! There seems to be great excitement in the South, over the election of Abraham Lincoln to the Presidency. I trust nothing serious will take place.

Enter EDWARD CLIFFORD, R.

Hunt. Ah, Edward; good morning.
Edward. Good morning, sir.
Hunt. Have you been down on 'change this morning?
Edward. Yes, sir; I have just come from there.
Hunt. How is cotton?
Edward. Gone up, a half to three-quarters. The excitement is very great, on account of the anticipated trouble with the South.
Hunt. Has Mr. Lockwood called this morning?
Edward. No, sir; he has not.
Hunt. By the way, Edward, you do not seem to esteem Mr. Lockwood very highly. I noticed last evening that you did not

treat him hardly with civility. You cannot but remember that ten years ago you came to my office a poor boy. I took you in my employ, and by your faithfulness and fidelity you have risen to your present position, confidential clerk to the largest cotton house in this city, and affianced husband of my daughter Maud.

Edward. For all your kindness to me, Mr. Huntington, I assure you I am deeply grateful, and I sincerely hope the trust and confidence you have placed in me may never be betrayed.

Hunt. My business relations with Mr. Lockwood have ever been the most pleasant. This is his first visit to our city, and I wish to extend to him that courtesy that is not only due him from our house as a business man, but as becomes his position as a gentleman. During my late visit to the South, he did everything in his power to make my stay agreeable, and I hope nothing will occur to mar the pleasure of this, his first visit to our city.

Edward. I confess I have a dislike to Mr. L., and though he may be what he seems, a perfect gentleman, I have formed a different opinion of him.

Hunt. What particular reason have you for forming other than a favorable one?

Edward. We sometimes form dislikes for people we know but little of; but to be frank with you, Mr. Huntington, I think he pays more attention to Maud than he should, knowing our relations to each other.

Hunt. Ha! ha! ha! Why, Edward, — jealous? I am surprised.

Edward. I think I have good reasons to be so. It is true Mr. Lockwood is your guest, and as such should treat Maud with the utmost respect; but for almost an entire stranger, I think he is too attentive to her.

Hunt. I think you misjudge him. It is quite natural in your position to feel as you do, I suppose; but I really think you make too much of the matter, as ——

Enter BILLY BRYANT, R.

Billy. Mr. Lockwood.   (*Exit.*)

Enter LOCKWOOD *smoking; bows coolly to* EDWARD. EDWARD *same to him.*

Lock. I trust I am not intruding.

Hunt. Oh, no; not at all. I am glad to see you. I have been expecting you all the morning.

Lock. I intended to call sooner, but have occupied the morning in writing letters to my friends and in reading the news. I see by the morning papers that cotton has advanced one-half to three-quarters. It is a fortunate thing for you that I made that last shipment just as I did, for if the cloud which now hangs o'er us, and threatens to envelop the country in a civil war, should not clear away, the prospects are that cotton will be exceedingly high, if not impossible to get.

Hunt. Is it your opinion that matters will prove so serious as to cause a war? God forbid that such a terrible thing should take place between brothers, as it were; although, if the South persists in carrying out the principles of secession that they have already put forth, it will be necessary for our government to take a firm stand, cost what it may.

Lock. (*Aside.*) Humph! (*Aloud.*) I hardly know what answer to make you, for, to tell you the truth, I have given but little thought to affairs of state, although there seemed to be considerable excitement in the South when I left there, which, after all, may blow over before anything serious takes place. (*Aside.*) But I hope not.

Hunt. Well, well; time will tell. (*To* EDWARD.) Edward, make out a check for five thousand dollars, to the order of Messrs. White, Woodward & Co., and step down there and settle our account with them.

(EDWARD *makes out check, and* HUNTINGTON *signs it.*)
(*Exit* EDWARD, R.)

Lock. Pardon me, Mr. Huntington, but it seems strange to me that you should have allowed this young man to become so intimate with your daughter. The position he holds in your house does not seem to me to warrant his assuming such familiarity. He is nothing but a clerk in your employ, and although he may hold a responsible position, still the very fact of his being but a clerk should have made you hesitate in giving him the hand of your daughter Maud.

Hunt. It may perhaps seem strange to you that Mr. Clifford should have so far worked himself into my affections as to have obtained my permission to woo my daughter, particularly as his station in life is so far beneath hers. But he has proved himself to be a young man worthy of confidence and esteem. He came to my office several years ago, a mere boy and an entire stranger. Won by his frank and honest appearance, I gave him employment. By his energy and faithful attendance to business he has worked himself to his present position. Having no friends in the city, I gave him a free invitation to my house, where he soon became acquainted with Maud and her brothers. An intimacy grew up between them which I rather encouraged than disapproved, having taken a strange liking to the young man. In short, he won Maud's love; and I am confident that in placing her in his care I am giving her to one who, though not her equal in wealth, is in every other way worthy of her.

Lock. I by no means intend to insinuate that he may not be a worthy young man, and capable of filling the position he holds in your office; but as to his being worthy of your daughter, excuse me, if I very much doubt it; but then, our ideas of such things are vastly different. We at the South would not tolerate such a matter. But aside from all this, without any intentions of injuring him in your estimation, there are other reasons for his not being worthy your daughter's love.

Hunt. Other reasons! Why, sir, what do you know of the young man?

Lock. I know but little, having seen him but a few times, and therefore am not perhaps competent to judge of his character; had it not been for something which transpired a few evenings ago, I should have hesitated in expressing my opinion of his unworthiness as I have. Last Monday evening, as you are aware, I attended the opera. After the performance, it being very stormy and disagreeable, I made all haste to reach your house; being unable to obtain a conveyance, I was obliged to walk. I had gone but a few blocks, when my attention was arrested by a man and woman who passed me, the woman apparently intoxicated. Something in the appearance of the gentleman led me to think I had met him before. My first thoughts were to continue on my way, without taking further notice of them, but curiosity or something or other, I know not what, led me to follow them. They passed through several of the principal streets, down into a locality, which, although unknown to me, showed in itself the nature of its inhabitants. Arriving at a filthy alley, they passed down, and were lost from my view. I stepped into a doorway, thinking that the young man might soon return, as I desired if possible to get a better view of him. After waiting some time, he made his appearance; as he passed by me, I found that my first suppositions were correct, and I fully identified him as Edward Clifford, your confidential clerk.

Hunt. Edward Clifford! impossible! You must be mistaken; your acquaintance with him is so limited, that it is very likely you have made a great mistake in the person.

Lock. Upon my honor as a gentleman, I assure you that the man I have spoken of was no other than Mr. Clifford. However, don't let this circumstance prejudice you against *him*, as *he* can *possibly* explain the matter satisfactorily.

Hunt. I am confident he can, as I have full faith in his honor and integrity. In the mean time, I will give this matter farther thought, and take the first opportunity to speak to him on the subject. (HUNTINGTON *looks at his watch*.) Half-past two, — I had no idea it was so late. Come, let us go to dinner.

Lock. You will please excuse me, Mr. Huntington, but I have an engagement which will prevent me from accepting your invitation. Present my compliments to your daughter, also my regrets that I am obliged to dine elsewhere to day.

Hunt. Very well, we shall expect you this evening.

Lock. Certainly! Good morning! (*Exit* LOCKWOOD, R.)

Hunt. There seems to be some mystery here; it certainly is very strange that Mr. Lockwood should meet Edward at such an hour of the night, in company with a woman of doubtful appearance, more especially after his having just left my daughter's presence. Either Mr. Lockwood must have made a fearful mistake, or Edward must be a consummate villain. And I cannot believe that. The only thing to be done, however, is to hear Edward's story and see what he has to say for himself. (HUNTINGTON *calls* NATHANIEL.)

Enter NATHANIEL, R.

Nath'l. Sir!

Hunt. Tell Edward, when he comes in, that I shall not return this afternoon. If Mr. Walker, the lawyer, calls, tell him I will see him to-morrow morning at nine o'clock.

Nath'l. Very well, sir! (*Exit* HUNTINGTON, R. *Nathaniel goes to table and takes up newspaper.*) I wonder what the news is; I have been trying all day to get hold of a newspaper. Holloa! what's this? (*Reads aloud.*) "Great excitement in Charleston, South Carolina. The people of the South preparing for war. Raising of the Palmetto flag on several of the public buildings; the American flag trailed in the dust." I was afraid it would come to this. It seem strange that a people should so far forget themselves as to turn against their own interests. (*Noise and boisterous laughter in outer office.*) There's those plaguey boys again up to their old tricks; the minute their employers back is turned, it's leave business, and go to playing. (NATHANIEL *looks out the door.*) Just as I expected, there's young Bryant on a stool playing tragedy, with Alphonse for au audience.

(BILLY BRYANT *recites outside.*)

"At midnight, in his guarded tent,
    The Turk was dreaming of the hour
When Greece, her knee in suppliance bent,
    Should tremble at his power."

Enter BILLY and ALPHONSE, R.

Billy. "To arms! To arms! they come! the Greek! the Greek!" (*Seats himself in chair, putting his feet on the table.*) I say, fellows, aint this a perfect home for a man? Nathaniel, Nathaniel, go to the office for the mail. Alphonso, go make out a check for ten thousand dollars. Nathaniel, bring me the morning paper. (NATHANIEL *brings paper.*)

Nath'l. Here's the morning paper, my young friend, and there's something in it you had better read. Perhaps you won't feel so much like shouting "To arms! To arms!" (*Shows* BRYANT *paper with paragraph.*)

Billy. (*Reads.*) "Great excitement in Charleston, South Carolina! The people of the South getting ready for war! Raising of the Palmetto flag on several of the public buildings! The American flag trailed in the dust!"

Nath'l. What do you think of that, sonny? You may have a chance to show your warlike spirit in something besides words.

Billy. We'll fight "till from our bones the meat be hacked;" won't we, Phony?

Alphonse. Not if I know myself, and I think I do. I never fought but once, and then I got licked; and I darsn't try it again.

Billy. Villain! wilt thou go back on me? Follow me, and do as I do.

Nath'l. Yes; follow you! If he did, the first thing would be to cut and run.

Billy.   "He who fights, and runs away,
        May live to fight another day."

I say, Nat, don't you think I would make a good actor?

Nath'l. I think if you paid more attention to business, and less to that infernal spouting, you would get along better in the world. Only day before yesterday Mr. Clifford wanted to know if there was any one sick in the outer office, when you were giving Alphonse a taste of your extraordinary dramatic abilities.

Billy. What a pity that two such intelligent persons as you and Ned should have such a fearful lack of appreciation. Phony is the only one in the office that has got any sort of taste for the fine arts. Never mind, I forgive you both. I dare say you never saw Forrest play "The Gladiator."

Nath'l. Can't say that I ever did.

Billy. That's what I thought. No wonder that you can't tell a good thing when you hear it. Now there's that place in the Gladiator where he says — "*Now by Jove, It is!*" but just wait a moment, and I will give it to you.

Nath'l. Oh! for mercy sake, don't.

Billy. Oh, it is no trouble at all. I know you are too bashful to ask me, so I will volunteer.

Alphonse. That's right, Billy; go ahead.

Billy. (*Puts chair on table.*) There, Phony, you get up there in the private box (*pointing to stool*). Nat, you set down there in the pit. Now, then, no applause; let me see. (*Starts from back and comes down furiously. NAT holds his hands over his ears.*)

Billy. "Now, by Jove, it is! These things do Romans! But the earth is sick of conquerors. There is not a man, not Roman, but is Rome's extremest foe. And such am I! Sworn from that hour I saw those sights of horror, While the Gods support me, To wreak on Rome such havoc as Rome wreaks — Carnage and devastation, woe and ruin! Why should I ransom, when I swear to slay? Begone!"—

During the above, EDWARD *and* HARRY *appear,* R.

Harry. (*Coming down.*) Bravo! Billy. Bravo! (ALPHONSE *slides down off the table, takes down chair, and writes furiously.* BILLY, *confused, goes to table, as if looking after something*).

Edward. Well, what is all this? You seem to be having a good time here all alone by yourselves, at the firm's expense; if you would like to have me, I will ask Mr. Huntington to turn his office into a theatre, and procure you some scenery.

Billy. You needn't mind it. I can do just as well without it.

Nath'l. Better get him a strait-jacket, sir.

(*Exit* NATH'L. R.)

Edward. Perhaps that would be more appropriate under the circumstances. It's a pity you can't attend to business, except when some one is watching you. You had better, both of you, go and finish up your accounts, instead of fooling away your time in such a manner.

Billy. Come, Phon., let's go; our talents aint appreciated here.

Alphonse. That's so!   (*Exit* BILLY *and* PHONY.)

Harry. (*Laughs.*) Now, what's the use blowing them up, Ned? You must remember William's weak propensities, and make some allowance for him.

Edward. I have no objections to his amusing himself, but this is not the proper place, Harry. I enjoy his nonsense at the armory or anywhere else as well as any one, but I cannot permit it here.

(HARRY *and* EDWARD *seated*, EDWARD *writing a letter.*)

Harry. By the way, Ned, speaking of the armory, don't forget there's a special meeting to-night, and it's necessary every member should be there.

Edward. So there is! I had almost forgotten it. My time has been so taken up the past day or two, that I have had but little chance to think of military matters.

Harry. No doubt your time is very much taken up; it could not be otherwise for a man in your situation; but come, haven't you got most through with that letter? We promised to meet Smith at Parker's at four o'clock, and it wants twenty minutes of it now; and I have got a little errand to do for Maud, before I go there.

Edward. Don't be impatient. There's plenty of time. Just a minute longer, Harry, and I will be through.

Harry. Well, hurry up, then; I don't want to stop here all the afternoon. Why don't you shut up your office in decent season, same as we do down to the bank?

(EDWARD *finishes letter, folding and sealing.*)

Edward. There, I am all ready now. Just step down to the post-office with me, until I leave this letter, and then we will keep our appointment with Smith.

Harry. Send Billy with the letter. What do you want to bother with it for?

Edward. Because it's of great importance, and I want to be sure that it gets into the office all right, so as to go by the five o'clock mail. Come, it will not put us out of the way two minutes.

Harry. All right. Go ahead! (*Exit* EDWARD *and* HARRY, R.)

SCENE II. — *Armory of the Bay State Rifles. Rack of muskets at back.* BILLY BRYANT, ALPHONSE *and members of the company discovered.* NATHANIEL, *as armorer, cleaning musket.*

Billy. Shine 'em up, Nat! Put in all the elbow-grease you can; I wouldn't wonder if we had to use them before long, if there is any truth in the latest reports from the South.

Nath'l. Yes; and you will find it somewhat different having to clean your own musket after using it, than having some one to do it for you. It's all very nice now, when you go out on parade, to come in and find a clean musket; but when you have to keep it clean yourself, it's another thing.

Alphonse. Do you suppose there will be a war, Nat; and if there is, do you suppose our company will go?

Nath'l. Can't say, Phony. I wouldn't be surprised if it finally came to war, and I would not wonder, in that case, if the boys received orders to go.

Billy. Perhaps that is what the special meeting is called for; but then, war hasn't been declared yet, and they can't call us out unless they do declare it.

Nath'l. Very true; but they can hold you in readiness for any emergency.

Fritz. Vell, I can't go; I am very sorry, but I can't.

Billy. Why, what is the matter with you, Dutchy?

Fritz. Someting the matter mit my feet; the toe-nail grows in, or sometings.

Billy. Something the matter with your feet? They are big enough to be healthy. One of your shoes would make a splendid tug-boat. If you only owned the ground your feet cover, you could set yourself up in the real estate business.

Fritz. Oh, vat's the matter mit you? Don't make me so much foolishness, always speedling about dose feet. I can't help it what I got big feet. Aint it, Swifty?

Thomas Swift. No, it aint your fault, Fritzy. Don't mind those fellows; they don't say half what they mean.

Fritz. Vell, I don't care someting much if I do wear number seventeen boots. I don't be spouting out all the time like Billy does, mit (*Recites and imitates*) "Is dat a cheese knife when I see, — now I don't see it, and den I saw it," and all such stuff like dat.

Swift. There's a hit for you, Billy!

Billy. How Swift you are to see it! Never mind, Fritzy, you are all right. If you had to hold Tom's body, you would want bigger feet than you have got now. (*All laugh.*) Well, Fritzy, we will call it square if you will give us a song. (FRITZ *sings Dutch song.*)

Enter CAPT. GREGG, NED *and* HARRY.

Alphonse. Holloa, boys! Here's the captain, with Ned and Harry.

NED *and* HARRY *shake hands with boys. Captain goes to his desk and takes papers out of his pocket. Members talking, etc.* CAPT. GREGG, *rapping:*

Capt. Gregg. You will please come to order. In pursuance with orders from headquarters, I have caused a special meeting to be called here this evening. That you may understand its object, I will read the order received. (*Reads order.*)

COMMONWEALTH OF MASSACHUSETTS.
HEADQUARTERS, BOSTON, Jan. 16, 1861.

GEN. ORDER NO. 4.—Events which have recently occurred and are now in progress, require that Massachusetts should be at all times ready to furnish her quota, upon any requisition of the President of the United States, to aid in the maintenance of the laws, and peace of the Union. His Excellency, the Commander-in-Chief, therefore orders:

That the commanding officer of each company of Volunteer Militia examine with care the roll of his company, and cause the name of each member, together with his rank and place of residence, to be properly recorded, and a copy of the same to be forwarded to the office of the Adjutant General.

Previous to which, commanders of companies shall make strict inquiry whether there are men in their command who, from age, physical defect, business, or family causes, may be indisposed to respond at once to the orders of the Commander-in-Chief, made in response to a call of the President of the United States, that they may be forthwith discharged, so that their places may be filled with men ready for any public emergency which may arise, whenever called upon.

Major-Generals Sutton, Morse and Andrews will cause this order to be promulgated throughout their respective divisions.

By command of his Excellency,

JOHN A. ANDREW,
Governor and Commander-in-Chief.
WILLIAM SCHOULER,
Adjutant Gen'l.

From this order you will see that we are to ascertain how many of this company are willing to hold themselves in readiness at a call from the Commander-in-Chief. Men, it is useless for me to inform you of the present state of the country. We are no doubt on the verge of a civil war; every report from the South shows us that it is inevitable; we must therefore look the matter squarely in the face, and let every man think well before giving his answer. The sacrifice you will be called upon to make will be a great one. Home, friends, and everything dear to you must be left behind, for the hardships and privations of the camp and field. I feel confident, however, that I can return to the Commander-in-Chief a unanimous vote of this company to respond at any time to his call in the defence of the country. I should like to hear the opinion of every member on this important subject.   (CAPT. GREGG *sits*.)

Edward. Mr. Commander.

Capt. G. Sergeant Clifford.

Edward. In my opinion, sir, the time has arrived when we should know whether we live under a constitutional government or not, and since our country is threatened, it is high time we should know who are its friends and who its enemies. It seems to me, with all due deference to the various public opinions that have been expressed, that our minds should be fully made up to the great occasion that now awaits us. I fully agree with you, sir, that the war is inevitable, and that it becomes us to give this matter our serious consideration. Our first duty is to our country; and though it may be hard to part with those near and dear to us at home, yet that duty must be fulfilled. I for one, sir, am ready and willing to place my name upon the roll.

Harry. Mr. Commander.

Capt. G. Orderly Sergeant Huntington.

Harry. I fully endorse the sentiments so ably expressed by Sergeant Clifford, and also stand ready to sign the roll.

Nath'l. Mr. Commander.

Capt. G. Private Foster.

Nath'l. I am much pleased to hear the opinions expressed by those preceding me. I have watched with great interest the actions of the South, and cannot but feel that it must come to war. I am sorry for it, but yet stand ready to-day, as I stood fifteen years ago, to support my country and my flag. I know full well the hardships and privations of a soldier's life; it is no boy's play. I have been through the Mexican war, and speak from experience. I am not an old man, though I am fifty years of age; and there is still life enough in me to fight for the old flag, and I should consider it a great honor if I might be allowed to place my name first on the roll.   (*Sits.*)

(*Applause by the Company.*)

Billy. Mr. Commander.

Capt. G. Corporal Bryant.

Billy. I, too, am ready to sign.

Alphonse. And I, too, sir.

Fritz. I goes me mit dem oder fellers.

Capt. G. I am glad you have expressed your opinions so freely and so nobly. Those of you who are now willing will step to the Orderly's desk, and sign your names. (*All come forward.* ORDERLY HUNTINGTON *hands the pen to* NATHANIEL.)

Billy. Three cheers for the Bay State Rifles! (*Cheers given.*)

TABLEAU.

Goddess of Liberty, with roll and flag.

MUSIC.

Viva la America.

SCENE III. — *Street scene. Enter* MR. LOCKWOOD, R., *smoking cigar.*

Newsboy. (*Outside.*) 'Ere's your Herald, Transcript, Journal — last edition — latest news from the South! (*Enter.*) Have a paper, sir?

Lock. Give me a Journal. (*Buys a paper.*)

Newsboy. (*Going out.*) 'Ere's your Herald. Last edition. Demand of the surrender of Fort Sumter by Governor Pickens of South Carolina. (*Exit* NEWSBOY, R.)

Lock. (*Reads.*) "Col. Hayne, of So. Carolina, as agent for Governor Pickens, reached Washington on the 12th, demanding the surrender of Fort Sumter, as essential to a good understanding between the two nations of South Carolina and the United States." So far so good. Matters appear to be coming to a crisis in the old Palmetto State. I must hurry up matters here, and get home again in time to be on hand for the first blow. My worthy friends here would not perhaps treat me as well if they knew I was colonel of a So. Carolina regiment of militia, and one of the prime movers in this rebellion; but even that might not affect them so much as the fact of my having shipped five thousand arms to the South. That was a good trick of mine, buying arms as agent for a Western State, and then running them to Charleston. It is very unfortunate for me that I was obliged to come here just now, but it had to be done. The old plantation is heavily mortgaged and pretty well run out; money must be had, especially at the present time; but how to get it — that is the question. Fortune deserted me at the gaming table, and I determined to try another scheme. Knowing that the old man Huntington was very favorably impressed with me. I resolved to visit him, get into the good graces of his daughter, marry her if possible, and in that way retrieve my lost fortune; but I find an unexpected barrier to my determinations in the person of this Clifford, to whom it seems Maud is engaged. But for all that, I shall not give it up tamely, and if it is possible to injure that young chap in the old man's estimation, why, I am just the one to do it.

(*Exit* LOCKWOOD, L.)

Enter BRYANT, ALPHONSE, FRITZ *and* SWIFT, L.

Alphonse. Well, we had an exciting meeting to-night, eh, boys? And the best of it is, all the fellows that were there signed the roll, and I guess the rest of the company will sign, too. At least, the captain says so.

Billy. I say, Phon, if our company goes, it will be rough on the old man. There will be Ned, Nat, you and I go out of the office. He had better shut up shop and go with us. Did you see Fritz's hand tremble, fellows, when he signed the roll? You are a dead Dutchman, sure, Fritz.

Fritz. (*Noisy.*) Who trembles my hand? Vat are you talking about? Aint you so funny, always picking on me? I pet you five hundred tollars my name is so much better written like yours.

Enter POLICEMAN. *Watches them.*

Swift. That's so, Fritzy. I saw Billy when he signed, and he left a big blot after his name, his hand shook so. (*Loud laughter.*)

Fritz. How's dat, Mr. Billy?

Police. Here, move on; you are making too much noise.

Billy. So am I.

Police. Well, now, I don't want any of your back talk. So jog along.

Fritz. (*Goes up to* POLICEMAN.) Say, Mr. Watch-house, vat's the matter mit you? Who owns this place? Aint I——

Police. Now, look here, if you don't move on, I will put you all in the lock-up.

Alphonse. Come on, Fritzy; let's go home.

All start out, SWIFT *walking slowly.* POLICEMAN *comes up behind him; gives him a push.*

Police. Come, get along there, Fatty; if you don't I'll help you.

Swift. I know; but what's the rush?

(*Exit* SWIFT *and* POLICEMAN.)

SCENE IV. — *Parlor in* HUNTINGTON'S *house.* — MAUD *and* MR. LOCKWOOD *discovered seated at table.*

Lock. Your father informs me that you intend crossing the Atlantic this spring.

Maud. That was our intention, but papa says we may be obliged to postpone it on account of the present state of the country. I am very sorry, for I had anticipated so much pleasure. Do you candidly believe that these difficulties cannot be settled, except by war? You are from the South, and ought to know the feelings of the people there.

Lock. True, Miss Maud, I ought, and I think I do know something of the sentiments of the Southern people. They are terribly in earnest, and unless the United States Government accedes to them the rights they demand, I fear civil war will be the result.

Maud. And should it finally come to war, I suppose you will give your services to your country, even though your home is in the South, for papa says you were a cadet at West Point, with brother Charles, and formerly held a commission as First Lieutenant in the regular army.

Lock. I assure you, Miss Maud, I have not yet made my decision. (*Aside.*) There's a fearful lie. I have tried to keep out of it as long as possible, for it is a hard matter to decide. I owe a debt of gratitude to my country for the many favors I have received from her; but I also owe to my native State loyalty and allegiance, and when the time comes, I hope to be found upon the right side. But let us change the subject for one more pleasant.

Maud. I agree with you, Mr. Lockwood. that the subject is an unpleasant one; but nevertheless we must look at it in its proper light. (EDWARD *appears at door*, c.) My grandfather was a soldier in the revolution, and helped to make this country a free and Independent Republic. He gave his life freely for her sake, and I have ever been taught that my first duty was to my country. I can hardly imagine there are people in this bright and happy land so misguided and narrow-minded as to wish to destroy it, and I earnestly hope that he whose hand is raised against his country's flag, may meet with a just and speedy punishment.

Edward. (*Coming down* c.) Nobly spoken, Maud, like a true American woman. Who can doubt the success of our cause when our women show such earnest devotion?

Lock. My young friend, have you looked at both sides of the question? The women of the South are equally as devoted to their cause as your Northern women, and are fully as eager to take part in this great work.

Edward. I care not took at both sides, sir; it is enough for me to know that my country is threatened and in great danger. There is but one side to *me*, and that is for the right. It is useless to argue the question. for I see but one course to pursue, and I have already expressed my willingness to sacrifice everything in my country's defence.

Maud. Why, Edward, has it come to that? Is there no hope that a peaceful settlement can be made without resorting to bloodshed.

Edward. I am afraid not. Already the first step has been taken, and orders have been received from the Commander-in-Chief for the militia of the State to hold themselves in readiness for a moment's notice, for any emergency. The Bay State Rifles have volunteered unanimously, and Harry and I have signed the roll.

Maud. O Edward, it will be hard to part with you; but I would not bid you stay when your country calls. And though it will make my heart ache, and cause me many bitter tears, yet will I wish you God-speed.

Enter JAMES, C.

James. (*Handing letter to* EDWARD.) Here's a letter, Mr. Bryant brought for you, sir. He said it came to the office after your departure, and he thought it might be of importance, so he came here with it. Miss Maud, your father would like to see you in the drawing-room.   (*Exit* SERVANT, C.)

Maud. I will be back directly.   (*Exit* MAUD, C.)

(EDWARD *opens letter and reads it. As he reads, shows signs. of surprise and emotion. Puts it in his pocket and it drops on the floor.*)

Edward. Please excuse me to Miss Maud, as this note demands my immediate attention. I will be back in half an hour.   (*Exit* EDWARD, C.)

Lock. (*Rising. Picks up letter.*) I wonder what correspondence Mr. Edward has to affect him so. (*Looks at letter.*) And a lady's handwriting, too. I suppose I ought to hand it back to him, but I think I will take a peep at it first. Perhaps it may be interesting.   (*Opens letter and reads aloud.*)

MY DEAR SIR: I am very sorry to trouble you, but can you not come to the house immediately. I am sure you will excuse me for presuming to ask your assistance, but I am in great distress. My darling little Minnie died this morning, of scarlet fever, and I have no earthly friend to call upon but you—you who saved me from starvation and placed me in this comfortable home, and gave me means to earn my daily bread. I am stricken down with sorrow and despair, and know not which way to turn. May Heaven in its infinite mercy bring comfort to my burdened soul.

Your afflicted friend,

LUCY CLIFTON.

So, so; Lucy Clifton. I suppose that is the woman I met with young Clifford on the evening I attended the opera. Well, there's nothing in that letter that interests me, so I—— Stop! Clifton, Clifford; yes, but there is something that interests me. Fortune has thrown this into my hands as an instrument to assist me in my schemes, and I will make good use of it, too. I'll change the letter so as to make it appear that this woman is Clifford's wife. I flatter myself I can imitate a lady's handwriting to perfection, and it would not be the first time I had forged somebody's name. It's a damnable deed, with such a subject as that letter contains, and a desperate game to play; but never mind, I have everything at stake, and something must be done. I will forge a letter, show it to Maud and her father, and then see if their worthy young friend can clear himself. (*Sits down; takes paper from table; hesitates; then takes paper from his pocket.*) There, I guess that will do. They can't catch me that way. Some one comes. (*Puts original letter in his pocket; folds up forged one, and puts it in the original envelope. Goes to another table and reads.*)

Enter Mr. Huntington, Maud *and* Harry, c.

Maud. Why, where's Edward?

Lock. He wished me to excuse him, as he had some important business to attend to in regard to a letter he had just received. He will be back in half an hour.

(Maud *and* Harry *retire back.*)

Lock. (*Coming down.*) Mr. Huntington, a word with you. Have you spoken with Mr. Clifford on that subject we were talking of? I mean in regard to my meeting him with that woman.

Hunt. No. I have not yet had an opportunity; but I intended doing so this very evening.

Lock. You will remember at that time I doubted the young man's worthiness. There is still farther proof that I was not mistaken. Read this. (*Handing him letter.*)

Hunt. Why, what is this? A letter directed to Edward. How came you by it?

Lock. Mr. Clifford, in his excitement, dropped it on the floor. I took the liberty to read it, and I feel that its contents will justify me in so doing.

(Harry *and* Maud *come down.*)

(Huntington *reads letter aloud.*)

My Dear Ned: Come to me immediately. I am in great distress. Our darling little Minnie has passed away. She died this morning of scarlet fever, raving and calling for her papa. I am stricken down with sorrow and despair, and know not which way to turn. If you love me, come to me at once.

Your heart-broken wife,

Lucy.

Hunt. (*Repeats.*) Your heart-broken wife, Lucy. Great heavens! What does this mean?

Maud. Edward married! It cannot be. (*Sinks into a chair.*)

Harry. Married! Humbug; it is a lie on the face of it.

Hunt. How do you know it's false? Explain this letter, then. It is plain enough to me that Edward has basely betrayed our confidence.

Maud. (*Going over to her father.*) Oh, father, you do not believe that Edward is so base. It seems to me like a fearful dream.

Hunt. Maud, he is no longer worthy of our regard or esteem. Henceforth with us he must be considered as a perfect stranger.

Enter EDWARD, c.

Edward. I hope you will excuse me, Maud, for my abrupt departure; but—— (*Looking round at them.*) Why, what has happened? Why do you all look at me so strangely? And Maud in tears. (*Steps towards her.*)

Hunt. Stop; how dare you intrude yourself into the presence of my daughter! You are a vile, contemptible scoundrel, and it is useless for you to attempt to carry out your base designs any farther. You are not fit to associate with respectable people. You are——

Edward. (*Thunderstruck.*) Hold, Mr. Huntington! What does this mean? What have I done that you should overwhelm me with such a tirade of abuse?

Hunt. What have you done? Edward, I did not give you credit for so much hypocrisy. I wonder that you can look honest people squarely in the face.

Edward. Before heaven I know not what you mean.

Hunt. Do you recognise this letter, sir? (EDWARD *takes letter; looks at envelope.*)

Edward. I do; it's mine. I must have dropped it.

Hunt. Very unfortunate for you. Are its contents true?

Edward. They are, sir; but I know - of nothing in them to justify you in using such abusive language to me.

Hunt. (*Sternly.*) You know of nothing in that letter that should justify me in addressing you as I have! Why have you left your wife alone in her great distress, to come here to practise your vile deceits?

(MUSIC—*Pianissimo—to end of scene.*)

Edward. (*Reading letter.*) Wife! Child! Why, sir, this letter is not mine. I received nothing like that.

Hunt. How ridiculous. A moment ago you acknowledged it was yours. Do you not know that woman?

Edward. I do, sir; but she is not my wife; she is a poor woman whom I have befriended, and——

Hunt. Stop, sir; do not add falsehood to your other sins. This letter was received by you not an hour ago, according to your own statement. It is unnecessary to have any further controversy on this subject. The letter explains itself. You will understand, sir, that all relations between you and my family are at an end. I bear you no ill-will, but from this time forward we are strangers.

(MAUD *starts to go to* EDWARD; *her father puts her back.*)

Edward. Maud, you do not believe this of me. Surely you cannot think me such a hypocrite.

Maud. O Edward, how could you so cruelly deceive us?

Edward. You, too, doubt me. Is there no one that will believe me?

Harry. Yes, Ned, I believe you. There's some fearful mistake here, which in time must be cleared away.

Lock. (*Aside.*) Yes; but it will be too late.

Edward. (*Clasping* HARRY'S *hand.*) I thank you, Harry, for your confidence. In time this mystery *will* clear away. (*To* HUNTINGTON.) I still persist in saying that that letter is not the one I received. Where it came from I know not. Would you but hear the truth, could you know the relationship between that woman and myself, you would bless me rather than spurn me from your door. The time will come, however (vile, contemptible scoundrel, though you call me), when it will be as freely opened to me as it was in former years.

TABLEAU. MUSIC—"*Out in the Cold World.*"

CURTAIN.

ACT II.

SCENE I.—*Same as Scene* VI, *Act* I.—MAUD *and* MR. HUNTINGTON *discovered.*

Hunt. Come, cheer up darling; do not look so sad.

Maud. Oh, father, the world seems like a dreary waste to me, from which everything bright and beautiful has vanished. Even life itself is a burden, and I long to be at rest.

Hunt. Do not say so, my child. You have something to live for, even though he whom you have trusted and loved has proved false.

Maud. True, father. Forgive me for speaking so; but I feel very sad to-day. Nearly three months have passed away since Edward left us, and during that time we have heard nothing of him; even Harry does not know of his whereabouts. When I look back into the past and think of the many happy hours we have spent together, of his frank and noble nature, his genial smile and pleasant word for all, it seems impossible that he should be such a heartless villain. I cannot realize it.

Hunt. Think no more of him; he is unworthy of so much feeling. Try and forget him.

Maud. Forget him. Ah! father, you know not what you say. You may as well ask me to blot from my memory the remembrance of my dear, dead mother, as to forget Edward; besides, something tells me he will one day be able to prove his innocence, and that even as he said on leaving us, the time will come when our doors will be as freely opened to him as they were in former years.

Hunt. Let that be as it may; there are other things I wish to say to you. Mr. Lockwood has asked the privilege of making you an offer of marriage. I granted this privilege, but told him I should in no way influence you. I believe Mr. Lockwood to be a worthy and honorable young man, and I think in case you should decide in his favor, he will be to you all that a lover or a husband should be.

Maud. Oh! father. How can you bring such matters before me now, when my heart seems too full for utterance. Do you think I can so soon forget Edward as to receive the advances of another. If you have given Mr. Lockwood the right to speak to me on this subject, I will receive him, but I tell you beforehand he will get but little encouragement.

Hunt. He is coming now. Remember, in no respect are you to do other than your own judgment tells you. You are mistress of your own heart, and in no way do I presume to dictate; but I believe it to be for your good to at least give him some hope.

(*Exit* HUNTINGTON, C.)

(MAUD *goes to table and sits.*)

Enter MR. LOCKWOOD, C.

Lock. Good evening, Miss Maud.

Maud. Good evening, Mr. Lockwood.

Lock. I wish to speak to you, Miss Huntington, on a matter of great importance to me. Your father has, no doubt, informed you what it is. I hope I am not too presumptuous in offering you my love at this time. I assure you I respect the lingering affection you must still have for Mr. Clifford, and deeply sympathize with you in your great trouble. I do not ask you to accept my offer unhesitatingly and without reflection. I only ask that you will give me hope. Can you not give me the assurance that at some future time you will look with favor upon me.

Maud. Mr. Lockwood, since you have seen fit to ask me this question, I will answer it in the same spirit of frankness that it was asked. As a friend of my father's, and as his guest, I honor and respect you, but other than a friend you can never be to me.

Lock. Ah! Miss Maud, surely this cannot be your final decision. You will not so cruelly cast aside the great love I bear you. Since I first met you I have loved you, and that love has grown so intense that I cannot live without you.

Maud. You forget, Mr. Lockwood, that you are comparatively a stranger to me. It is barely three months since you first made my acquaintance, and in that short time you could hardly be able to form a favorable opinion of me, much less have learned to love me.

Lock. You are mistaken there. My opinion was formed of you ere I had been in your presence two hours, and it is needless for me to state that it was a favorable one. Will you not give me some encouragement, be it ever so slight, that I may not be doomed to utter disappointment. Only tell me that I am not distasteful to you, and that you do not look coldly upon my suit, and I will wait patiently until such time as you may choose to give me a decided answer.

Maud. I need no time, sir, to give you my decided and final answer. I shall be most happy at all times to call you my friend, and as such you will always be welcome here, but my love was given to another years ago, and strange as it may perhaps appear to you, I still cling to the first love; but even were I free to accept the offer you have been pleased to make me, there is another reason why I would reject it. I would never give my hand to any man who, in the hour of his country's peril, could for a moment hesitate as to what course to pursue.

Lock. Were I to pledge you my word that in case of war I would not take up arms against the government, would you then give me any encouragement?

Maud. It is your duty, sir, to be ready at any time to defend your country from danger, for her sake alone; and I should very much doubt the strength of your loyalty, if it depended upon my answer, as to which side you should take in the coming contest. I beg of you, Mr. Lockwood, do not refer to the subject again.

Charles. (*Outside.*) You needn't mind about ushering me in; I guess I can find the way.

Maud. As I live, there's brother Charles!

Lock. (*Aside.*) Charles Huntington here! What ill luck brings him home at this time? (*Retires up.*)

Enter CHARLES *and* MR. HUNTINGTON, C. MAUD *runs to meet* CHARLES.

Maud. Why, my dear brother, where did you come from? I am delighted to see you! You must be very tired and hungry, Charles. I will go and see to getting you some refreshments, and preparing your room. (*Exit* MAUD, C.)

Charles. I have just arrived from Charleston, South Carolina.

Hunt. Just arrived from Charleston? Why, the last we heard from you was in Alabama.

Charles. I was in Montgomery until the formation of the Confederate Government, but after that I left for Charleston, as it was getting rather uncomfortable for a loyal man in that section of the country. I found it but little better in Charleston, and barely escaped from there with my life. Business is entirely suspended at the South. The entire people are up in arms, and everything has a martial appearance. Already the forts around Sumter are making preparations to shell it, and it will be only a matter of two or three days before the first shot will be fired, unless our government surrenders the fort.

Hunt. Then there is no hope for a peaceful settlement of these difficulties, for the government would not listen to any proposal of surrender to a band of armed men, whose object is to rend asunder the bonds of union, and form a new government on the basis of State rights. There is no doubt but what this rebellion will be speedily suppressed, and the instigators of it meet with a just punishment. (*Looking towards* MR. LOCKWOOD.) Excuse me, Mr. Lockwood, I had quite forgotten you were here. Charles, this is an old friend of yours, — a classmate at West Point.

Lock. (*Coldly.*) I am happy to meet Mr. Charles Huntington.

Charles. (*Surprised.*) Guy Lockwood! I wish I could return the compliment! Father, I was not aware you were acquainted with Mr. Lockwood.

Hunt. Oh, yes, I have had dealings with him in business for the past seven years. He is my largest consignor of cotton in the South, and is just now making us a visit, partly for business, and partly for pleasure.

Charles. Humph! His business must be of a very urgent nature, that keeps him away from his friends when his services are needed so much; or else he is enjoying himself here among the mudsills so well that he cannot tear himself away.

Lock. I don't understand the meaning of your language, sir. Do you intend to insult me?

Charles. You don't understand me? Well, I propose to make

myself understood, perfectly, not only to you, but to my father. I have just come from Charleston, where I met with a very warm reception. I was obliged to leave there very suddenly, on account of my principles not being exactly in accordance with those of the fire-eaters there; but I remained long enough to find out a few things not very favorable to your character. The very day I reached there, the city was jubilant over the arrival of a large quantity of arms, that had been smuggled from the North. These arms, they said, had been purchased by one Guy Lockwood, Colonel of the 15th South Carolina Regiment, and one of the leaders in this rebellion, who had been commissioned by the Confederate States' Government to procure them, and who, I heard, was still in the North. Is it clear to you now, or do you wish me to go into further details? The best thing you can do, is to hurry back to the South before it is too late; for if I but give the information I have concerning you to the proper authorities, you may be obliged to stop here rather longer than you intended.

Hunt. I am astonished at your words, Charles. Mr. Lockwood, is this true what my son has just told us?

Lock. It must be true if he says so. He, of course, must know all about it; and were I to deny it you would not believe me.

Charles. You are right, they would not; for I can bring proof of what I have said, if necessary. Your little game is blocked here, and I don't intend to have you impose upon my father any longer.

Lock. (*Speaks to* MR. HUNTINGTON.) I am surprised that you permit this insult to pass unnoticed, even though it comes from your son. I consider it beneath me to make any reply to his well-fashioned story, but shall take the first opportunity to make him answer for it. I am deeply indebted to you, sir, for your kindness to me in making my visit here so pleasant, and to Miss Maud for her agreeable company. I am very sorry that the sudden appearance of this boisterous fellow will compel me to shorten my stay, but under the circumstances I can remain here no longer. I think, after all, I will act upon his suggestion, and return to the South.

Hunt. You do not mean to say that you intend to take part with the Southern Confederacy in this struggle?

Lock. That is just my intention, sir. I may as well own up to it at once, for I am not ashamed of it. I have given my whole heart and soul to the cause of the South, and will do everything in my power to aid and assist her. You will find to your sorrow, gentlemen, that this will be a long and bloody war, in which the South must be victorious. (*To* CHARLES.) If, during the struggle, the fortunes of war permit us to meet again, be it upon the battle-field or elsewhere, rest assured I shall spare no pains to remind you of this insult. I wish you a very good-morning.

TABLEAU OF CHARACTERS. SCENE CLOSES.

SCENE II. — *Street scene.* — *Ringing of bells and firing of guns, as if in the distance.* — *Men hurrying to and fro.* — *Enter* AL-PHONSE *and* BILLY BRYANT, R., *talking excitedly, and go across stage.*

Fritz. (*Enters on* R.) Say, Billy, what makes all the noise for, ain't it? Vat's the trouble mit dose bells? Where is the fire?

Bryant. Fire! What are you talking about, Dutchy? Aint you heard the news?

Fritz. What news?

Bryant. Why, Fort Sumter has gone up. The war has begun, and the President has called for seventy-five thousand men. We are just going down to the armory now.

Fritz. So help me gracious, is dat so? You don't told me!

Alphonse. Come along with us. Our company has orders to report to-morrow morning, and we are going down now to see the boys, and find out all the particulars. Your name is on the roll, and of course you will go with the company.

Fritz. Of course I goes. You can count on me, every time. Aint dat so, Billy?

Bryant. I suppose it is, Fritz. You are fearfully brave, especially where there is a charge to be made on pretzels and lager.

Enter SWIFT, R., *running, very much out of breath.*

Swift. I say, fellers, why didn't you stop for me when I halloed to you? I have been trying to catch up with you for the last ten minutes. Where are you going? Down to the armory?

Alphonse. Yes; aint you?

Swift. Yes; but what's your hurry? You fellers go as if you were sent for. Let's take it easy.

Bryant. Take it easy! This is a pretty time to talk about taking it easy! Where's your patriotism? Didn't you hear the guns firing and the bells ringing?

Fritz. Yes. Don't you hear the bells firing, and guns ringing?

Swift. Well, let 'em ring. No use running your legs off, is it?

Bryant. Swift thou art in name, but slow in nature. Come on, fellows!

Fritz. You go me first, we all follow after.

(*All exit, noise ceases.*)

Enter CHARLES *and* HARRY, R., *conversing.*

Charles. And you say you have seen nothing of him since that time, and have been unable to find out where he is?

Harry. I have neither seen him, nor heard anything from him since that night. After we left the house, we walked down town together. Edward seemed very much affected, but did not wish to converse on the subject, although he thought father had done him a great injustice in not giving him a chance to vindicate himself. I reassured him of my confidence, and then left him, expecting to see him the next day; but I have searched the city over, been in every place he would be likely to be in, but to no purpose. I endeavored to find out where this woman lived, but was unsuccessful. I think he must have left the city.

Charles. Very strange. I wish it were possible to find him, for I think he could make matters clear, at least to us.

Harry. I am sure he could. Let's take a walk down to the armory. We are ordered off to-morrow, and no doubt some of the boys are there now. (*Start out.*)

Enter EDWARD.

Harry. Ned Clifford! Where on earth did you drop from, and where have you been all this time. Charles and I were just talking about you.

Edward. (*Shakes hands with* HARRY.) I am glad to see you, Harry. Charles, this is, indeed, a pleasure; it is a long time since I saw you last.

Harry. Now explain yourself. Where have you been for the past three months?

Edward. After leaving you that night, I went to the hotel. I had no definite idea of what I should do, but my mind was fully made up to leave the city the next morning. I took the train for New York, where I remained until the President's call for troops. I then started for Boston again, knowing that our company would be ordered off.

Charles. Edward, I have heard the whole story of your troubles, and I agree with Harry that you are entirely innocent of the charges brought against you.

Edward. Thank you, Charles, you give me courage by your kind words. Heaven only knows how I have suffered from this injustice! Had your father but been willing to listen to me, I could have easily convinced him there was no truth in the matter, but as he saw fit to condemn me without giving me a chance to vindicate myself, I must abide the issue and await patiently until such time as he himself shall find me innocent. Oh! had Maud but believed in me, as you have done, I could have borne my burden without a murmur. I could have even forgiven your father for his rude treatment of me, knowing that I still possessed her love.

Harry. Cheer up, Ned. I am half inclined to believe that Maud does not think as ill of you as you imagine. But why don't you get this woman, bring her to our house, and prove to them your innocence?

Edward. I could do so, but I prefer to have them find it out themselves. I have a request to make of you, Harry; before you go, I wish to speak to your father on this subject. Will you obtain me an interview?

Harry. I will, Ned, and do anything in my power to assist you.

Charles. And so will I.

Harry. Won't you walk down to the armory with us, Ned? We were just on our way there when we met you.

Edward. I shall be happy to accompany you.

Charles. Do, Ned, and on the way give us further particulars in regard to this matter.

(*Exeunt,* L.)

SCENE III. — *Friends congregated on the streets to witness the departure of the troops.* (MAUD, MR. HUNTINGTON, CHARLES, MRS. DE PEYSTER, POLICEMAN, NEWSBOY, *and others.*)

Hunt. Do the boys seem to be in good spirits, Charles?

Charles. They do, sir. I came from the armory not half an hour ago, and they are wild with excitement. Ned Clifford arrived from New York yesterday, and the warm reception he received must be particularly gratifying to him under the present circumstances.

Maud. (*Much agitated.*) Will he be here with the company?

Charles. He will, and I think it your duty to at least bid him good-bye.

Hunt. Most assuredly we will. If a cheering word from us will do him any good, we will not withhold it.

(*Cheers and drums at a distance.*)

Enter Troops headed by CAPT. GREGG, L. C.

Capt. Gregg. Halt! Front! Order Arms! Rest!

(ALPHONSE *and* BRYANT *come down.*)

Alphonse. Here we are, mother, all ready to go.

Mrs. De Peyster. Alphonse, my darling boy, may Heaven bless you and keep you from all harm. 'Tis hard to say good-bye, but I will not discourage you. I will try and be cheerful and wish you a safe return to me. (CAPTAIN GREGG *comes down.*)

Alphonse. Mother, this is Captain Gregg.

Capt. Gregg. I am happy to meet you, madam ——

Mrs. De Peyster. Captain, I give my boy into your charge. Take good care of him and keep him from all evil, for he is my only son. Alphonse, take this Bible; read it my boy, for it will bring you comfort in your hours of trial. (*Puts ring on his finger.*) I give you this ring as a talisman. Whenever you are tempted to do wrong, look at it, and remember mother put it on your finger.

Corp'l. Bryant. We will take good care of him, Mrs. De Peyster; don't give yourself any uneasiness on that score. (*Retire and talk dumb-show.*) (HARRY *comes down.*)

Harry. Father, Ned wishes to speak a few words with you and Maud; will you not grant him this privilege, for my sake?

Hunt. Certainly, Harry, we will give him our best wishes. (HARRY *goes back, brings down* EDWARD, *and then goes to* Charles.)

Edward. Mr. Huntington, notwithstanding your having forbidden me to speak to you or Maud again, I desire to say a few words before my departure. Will you do me the favor to call at this address (*handing him card*)? You may, perhaps, obtain such information as will convince you, as I have not been able to do, that you have done me a great wrong.

Hunt. I will do as you request, Edward, and if I have wronged you, be assured I shall not rest easy until I have made amends for my conduct. You deserve my thanks, for so nobly responding to your country's call, and for that reason, if no other, I wish you God speed. (*Gives his hand.*) (Mr. HUNTINGTON *retires to* CHARLES *and* HARRY.)

Edward. Maud, in a few moments I must leave you, perhaps never to return. When I placed my name upon the roll, three months ago, to hold myself in readiness for any emergency, I little thought our parting would be like this. I had looked forward to this hour with the feeling that I should be cheered on my way with your love and blessing. I have no father or mother, brother or sister, to say good-bye, and wish me a safe return, but I could have forgotten that, had your love been spared to me. Have you not a cheering word for me before I go? It would repay me somewhat for the sufferings of the past three months.

Maud. Heaven knows you wrong me, dear Edward, if you think I do not love you. I, too, have suffered since our parting. Your assurance that you were innocent of this dreadful charge has found a place in my heart, and I cannot let you go away with one single feeling of doubt that my love for you is not as deep as ever. Though you have no father or mother, sister or brother to cheer you on your way, yet my love shall supply their places. May the kind Father guard and protect you, and keep you from all harm. (*Drums beat.*)

Capt. Gregg. Fall in!

(*Friends bid the soldiers good-bye, and the boys take their places in the ranks. Captain gives orders : Attention, Company ! Shoulder arms ! Right face ! Forward, march ! Troops march around stage, and exit* R. B. *Friends retire back, cheering and waving handkerchiefs. Exeunt all but policeman and newsboy. As the policeman is going out,* R., *newsboy pulls his coat-tails. Policeman turns to chase newsboy out,* L., *and runs into* FRITZ, *who enters* L., *out of breath, with gun in one hand, and large Bologna sausage in the other.*)

Fritz. (*Hitting policeman on head with Bologna.*) Gone away, old useless! If you don't I'll shoot myself.

Police. If you calculate to go away with Captain Gregg's company, you had better be going, without any more chat.

Fritz. Mind my own business. (*Takes a huge bite from the sausage, and exits* R.)

Enter SWIFT, L., slowly.

Swift. Say, have the soldiers gone?

Police. Yes, lightning; and have got into battle by this time.

SWIFT *goes out* R., *slowly, speaking as he goes.*

Swift. Well, then, I will hurry up and catch 'em.

Police. Do. You will probably overtake them by the time the war ends.

Exeunt SWIFT R., POLICEMAN L. *Scene changes.*

SCENE IV. — LUCY CLIFTON's *room. Enter* LUCY, R., *with work.*

Lucy. (*Laying down her work.*) There! that is the fourth garment I have finished to-day, and with the others already done will make a dozen. How kind in Mr. Clifford to obtain me such good work, and with such nice people! They really take a great interest in me, but I suspect it is more on his account than on my own. It seems very strange that he does not come here. Since the night little Minnie died I have not seen him. I hope nothing has happened to him. (*Knock at door.*) That must be Mrs. Peters, who lives on the second floor. Come in.

Enter MR. HUNTINGTON, MAUD, *and* CHARLES.

Lucy. (*Rising.*) Strangers! I beg your pardon for not opening the door. Pray be seated.

Hunt. Is your name Lucy Clifton?

Lucy. It is, sir.

Hunt My name is Samuel Huntington, and this is my daughter Maud, and my son Charles. We called to see you, at the request of your husband, who has just left Boston in the Bay State Rifles.

Lucy. My husband! I don't understand you, sir. I am a widow. My husband died six years ago. You must have made a great mistake.

Hunt. I think not. I refer to Mr. Edward Clifford.

Lucy. Mr. Edward Clifford? What do you mean, sir? What reason have you for supposing he is my husband? My name is not Clifford, but Clifton.

Hunt. It makes but little difference in regard to the name. My object in asking you is this. Mr. Clifford was engaged to my daughter until three months ago. One evening, while at my house, a letter was handed him which appeared to affect him very much. During his excitement he dropped it. It was picked up and handed to me, as the information it contained was of the utmost importance. That letter came from you, and was signed, as you can see (*handing her the letter*), your loving wife, Lucy.

(LUCY *takes the letter, reads it.*)

Lucy. I did write a letter to Mr. Clifford, and probably on the very evening to which you refer. This letter, sir, is not the one I sent, although it is very nearly like it, except that I did not sign myself your loving wife, Lucy.

(HUNTINGTON *returns to* CHARLES, *expresses astonishment.*)

Maud. (*Crosses to* LUCY.) And do you truly say that Edward Clifford is not your husband?

Lucy. Sincerely I do.

Maud. Then what relationship exists between you?

Lucy. He is my benefactor, and a true friend to me. But for him I should have perished from starvation and exposure.

Maud. Is it possible? How strange that Edward never mentioned you to us!

Lucy. Not so very strange. Mr. Clifford is not a man to trumpet forth his actions to the world; he is satisfied with having relieved a suffering fellow-creature from distress, and therefore had no desire to speak of it, not even to you, miss, of whom he has often spoken, and always in terms of highest praise.

Maud. O father! I fear we have done Edward a great wrong. (*To* LUCY.) Will you tell us the circumstances of your becoming acquainted with him, and how he relieved you from want?

Lucy. I will, with pleasure. But, first, I will give you a little history of my life. I was married ten years ago to Mr. John Clifton, of New York. We lived happily together for four years, when he was taken from me, leaving me with an infant child, alone in the world. He left me a little property, which, with careful management, lasted until a few months ago. I was then taken sick, and being unable to work we were reduced to extreme want. One night last January, after having been without food all day, I wandered forth into the streets, determined, if I could obtain help in no other way, to beg. It was a bitter cold night, the storm beat down furiously, and the streets were almost deserted. Men hurried by me, and to my entreaties for help, only buttoned their coats tighter and passed on. In my despair I threw myself down on the sidewalk to die. Just then Mr. Clifford came along, and, seeing me, stopped and spoke to me. I told my story, and he took pity on me. He took me back to my miserable home, procured me fire and food, and left me, promising to call and give me further assistance next day.

Maud. (*In tears.*) How noble! How like his dear, generous nature! And to think that we should have believed him such a villain! Oh, I can never forgive myself for having listened to it, much less believed it!

Hunt. I begin to think we were rather hasty, and I am vexed with myself for not having given him a chance to tell his story. It would have saved the poor boy many hours of pain and suffering; but go on with your story.

Lucy. True to his promise he called upon me the next day, cheered me by his kind words, and made the future look brighter to me than it had before since my husband's death. He removed me from the miserable place I was then living in to this comfortable home, procured me good work, and at much better pay than I could have obtained without his assistance. Quite often he called here to see if we were comfortably situated, but since the night I wrote him I have seen nothing of him, and now you say he has gone to war.

Hunt. Yes, he left yesterday, and before going he wished us to come and see you, saying that you could explain matters to our satisfaction. I am now thoroughly convinced that you are not Edward's wife, for I have listened to your story with interest, and believe it to be true, and if I could only account for that letter I should be perfectly satisfied.

Lucy. Can you think of no one who would have an object in injuring Mr. Clifford, and who might have written the letter?

Charles. (*Starting suddenly, as though struck with an idea.*) Yes. Let me see this terrible letter, if you please. I have never seen the cause of all this mischief before. (LUCY *hands the letter to* CHARLES; *he reads it, then carelessly turns it over and starts*). Father, did you read the whole of this letter?

Hunt. (*Taking letter.*) Why, yes, of course I did.

Charles. Both sides of it? Turn it over, please.

Hunt. (*Turns over letter, and reads*): "Send shipment of Sea Island Cotton and oblige, yours truly, SAM'L HUNTINGTON." (*All listen eagerly.*) Why, I have never seen that before!

Charles. Do you remember writing such a letter.

Hunt. I do, some six months ago, to Mr. Lockwood.

Charles. Exactly. There you have the mystery cleared up, as it might have been months ago, if you had read the whole letter.

Hunt. I understand. You wish to imply that Mr. Lockwood wrote that letter, and put it in the envelope in place of the original.

Charles. Right. It is as plain to my mind as though I saw him do it.

Maud. Do you think he would do such a thing as that?

Charles. No; I don't think so, I know it. You don't know that man as I do. He is capable of anything, no matter how rascally it may be.

Hunt. But what could be his object in injuring Edward?

Charles. I don't know, unless he was after Maud, and wished to get rid of Edward in that way.

Hunt. What could I have been thinking of that this did not occur to me before? It is all clear now, — Mr. Lockwood's endeavoring to make me believe that Edward was not worthy of Maud, his being so ready to show me the letter, and his appearing to be so gratified at the result. I wonder at my being so blind.

Charles. So do I, but not so much at you, as at Maud. Her love should have kept her faith in him proof against all calumnies.

Maud. Charles, do not condemn me. I was so overcome by what that letter contained, that I had no time to think. Since then I have thought it all over, and my heart told me, just what has been proved here, that he could clear himself. Father, now that I know Edward is true, I can stay at home no longer. With your permission I am going to Washington, volunteer my services as a nurse, and take an active part in this rebellion.

Lucy. Take me with you, I have nothing to keep me at home, and I, too, long to take an active part in this war. Will you not let me go with you? and together we will work to relieve the suffering of those who are so nobly fighting for our country's defence.

Maud. I should be delighted to have you go. Call at my house to-morrow, and we will talk this matter over.

Hunt. Mrs. Clifton, if there is any assistance I can render you, or if you require my services in any way, don't hesitate to call upon me.

Lucy. Thank you, I know of nothing now. I only wish that this affair could have been cleared up before Mr. Clifford went away.

Hunt. No more than I do. We will bid you good morning, and remember, if there is anything you need, do not be afraid to speak of it.

Maud. Don't forget to-morrow. (*Exit* HUNTINGTON, MAUD, *and* CHARLES.)

Lucy. (*Goes to table, sits, and takes up work.*) What a very strange affair! And to think that I should be interested in it, too. I am surprised that Mr. Huntington and Maud, knowing Edward as they do, should not have seen through this trick as easily as Mr. Charles did. (*Drops her work.*) Dear me, how sleepy I am! My good, kind benefactor, would that you could know this night how fully you are exonerated from all blame! Heaven spare your life and shield you from the enemies' bullets, for where the fight is the thickest, there I am sure you will be found. (*Falls asleep.*)   MUSIC. — *Pianissimo.*

ANIMATED TABLEAU (AT BACK.)

(LUCY'S VISION.)

ACT III.

SCENE I. — *Camp.* — *Row of tents on each side, with wall tent at back.* — *Bugle sounds " Reveille " outside.* — *Drums beat same on stage.*

Ord. Serg. Huntington. (Coming out of his quarters.) Turn out, boys, for roll call. (*Soldiers come out of tents and form line, all but* SWIFT *and* FRITZ. *Private* HARRIS, *in shirt sleeves.*)

Ord. Serg. H. Harris, go back to your quarters and get your blouse. (*Calls roll.*) Serg. Clifford (here); Serg. Foster (here); Serg. Brown (on guard); Corp. Bryant (here); Corp. Benson (here); Corp. Henshaw (on guard); Corp. Jenning (here; Private Butler (here); Priv. Chittenden (on picket); Chester (here); De Peyster (here); Dudley (here); Davis (here); Farquharson (here); Harris (here); Picket (here); Pulsifer (here); Raymond (here); Rogers (here); Ranson (on guard); Speighelhaulter (*asleep in his quarters;*) Swift (*coming out of his quarters, buttoning up his blouse, and in his stocking feet*) (here); Private Swift, go back to your quarters and put on your shoes; Private Sampson (on guard); Private Thompson (here); Tewksbury (here). (*Ord. Serg.* HUNTINGTON *details guard*). Serg. Foster, Corp. Benson, Privates Picket, Pulsifer, Raymond and Rogers. Camp Guard. Corp. Bryant, Privates Dudley, De Peyster and Davis for police duty. Right face, break ranks, march. (*Troops go to their tents.*) Corp. Bryant, you will excuse privates Dudley and Davis from police, and put in their places privates Swift and Speigelhaulter. (*Serg. H. goes to his tent.*)

Corp. Bryant. (Goes to Private DAVIS' *tent, and to next tent.*) Private Davis, you are excused from police. Private Dudley, you are excused from police. (*Goes to* FRITZ' *tent.*) Dutchy, you and Fatty Swift are put on police.

Swift. What's that for?

Fritz. Dat ish played out. I vas on polices yesterday. I have got me orful sick. I am going up to see the sturgeont, when the sick call comes round mit the drum.

Corp. Bryant. Well, you will have to go to the Orderly; I can't excuse you.

(*Orderly comes down.* SWIFT *and* FRITZ *go to him.*)

Swift. Say. Sergeant, I wasn't detailed for police. I was on guard yesterday.

Fritz. I can't go me on polices; I got sick mit my stomach. Oh, I feel so bad!

Ord. Sergt. H. You are both put on police for not being at roll-call this morning.

Swift. I was at roll-call. sergeant.

Ord. Sergt. H. Yes, I know you was, after the roll was called.

Fritz. Sergeant. I was sicker mit my stomach, as all night I couldn't crawl me out mit the tent.

Ord. Sergt. II. You were all right at the cook-house, last night.

Fritz. I knows, but dis is since that.

Ord. II. Well, you must fall in at the sick call, and if the Doctor excuses you from duty, all right.

Fritz. Vell, I goes mit the sick doctor, when he calls mit the bugle, (*Rubbing his stomach.*) Oh, mine Got in Himmel, Ise so sick! (*Breakfast call sounds on bugle, men fall in with plates and tin dippers.*)

Fritz. (*Forgetting his sickness.*) Breakfast; veres my dishes. (*Runs and gets his dishes and crowds into head of line. Company march out and get rations, and return to quarters.* FRITZ, SWIFT *and* ALPHONSE *come together, and sit down in front of their tent,* FRITZ *eating furiously.*)

Alphonse. Fritzy, you don't eat much like a sick man. I guess you feel better. I should hate to have to feed you if you *were* well.

Fritz. Vell, I feels a little mite better. Ven I eats I always makes me better.

Swift. Say, Fritz, go light on that. that's all you'll get to day.

Fritz. Don't I got me no dinner?

Swift. Nary a dinner. The cook told us last night they was going to issue rations in the morning for all day.

Fritz. (*Dropping his knife.*) Den I gone right off and change my boarding house. If I can't got me three meals a day, I go me back home again. (*Holding up hard tack.*) You think that last me all day.

Bryant. Judging from the sick night you had, and the way you have commenced, I don't think it will.

Fritz. What's de matter wid you, Smarty? Whose stomach is this what I got to feed, ain't it?

(*Bugle sounds sick call.*)

(*Three or four men fall in.*)

Brant. There you go Fritzy; fall in with the lame, sick and lazy.

Fritz. I ain't got me done mit my preakfast yet. (*Fills his mouth full and puts the rest under his blouse, and while he is marching out, keeps taking bite on the sly.*)

FRITZ *and other sick men come back,* FRITZ *looking thoroughly disgusted.*

Alphonse. Did the doctor excuse you?

Swift. Did he give you any medicine to cure you?

Fritz. Don't speak mit me.

Bryant. What's the matter, Dutchy? What did he say to you?

Fritz. Vell, I went up there, and he told me vat vas the matter mit me, and I said I feel very bad of my stomach, so he gave me sometings nasty and told me to took it. and den I vould veel me better. I took it, and dunder and blitzen wasn't it dirty; and den I thought he would say, go back and lay down mit your tent.

Alphonse. Well, what did he say?

Fritz. Ven I took the stuff he says, man, you feel all right; you can go back and report for duty. If I ever catch me mit that doctor ven I get home, I makes him take something vat he don't like.

Corp. Bryant. Well, fall in for police duty.

ALPHONSE, SWIFT, *and* FRITZ *go down to cook-house, come back, and sweep company street. Bugle calls for guard mounting.*

Ord. Serg't. II. Fall in for guard mounting. (*Men detailed for guard, fall in, march off.*)

Enter PEDLER *with two baskets, apples and oranges.*

Pedler. Here's your nice oranges and apples! (*Boys all crowd around him.* SWIFT *and* FRITZ *get up nearest to the man.*)

Swift. How much do you ask for apples?

Pedler. Five cents apiece.

Swift. Got any little ones for a cent? (*Soldier reaches behind the man, and takes an apple. Pedler turns round.*)

Pedler. Here! what are you doing there? (*As he turns round some one pushes* FRITZ *over the basket, and the apples and oranges roll around the stage. Boys all scramble for them.* FRITZ *picking himself up.*)

Fritz. Oh, vat's the matter? Say, Swifty, give us a bite of that apple.

Pedler. Now, who is going to pay me for that fruit? (*Two or three of the boys grab him and put him out, and then throw his basket after him.*)

Enter PEDLER *and* CAPT. GREGG.

Capt. Gregg. Which one of you was it that tipped over the man's basket?

All say. It was Dutchy!

Fritz. 'Twasn't me! Some feller pushed me and tumbled me down. I could't help it. You fellers are always laying everything on me. So help me General Butler, captain, I did not get a bite!

Capt. G. (*Turns to* PEDLER.) It will be pretty hard work, my man, to find out any particular one who did it. The whole company are to blame, and if I punish one I must punish the whole. I will take care it does not occur again.

Pedler. But who is to pay me for my apples and oranges?

Capt. G. How much were they worth?

Pedler. Five dollars.

Bryant. Don't you give it to him, captain. He did not have a dozen of any kind. Give him a half a dollar, and let him go.

All say. That's so! Kick him out! (*All make a rush toward him.* CAPTAIN *orders them back.*)

Capt G. Stop, boys! no violence. My good man, you had better get out of this before you get hurt. (PEDLER *exits hurriedly,* R.)

Enter private CHITTENDEN *with a contraband. Boys gather around him.*

Harris. Where did you get that crow-foot, Henry?
Chit. Picked him up on the outpost. He says he wants to be a Yankee.
Bryant. Well, then, he has got to be whitewashed.
Pompey. I wouldn't be de first whitewashed nigger in de camp. (CAPT. G. *comes out of his quarters.*)
Capt G. What have you there, private Chittenden?
Chit. Contraband, sir, from the outposts. He wanted to come into our camp.
Capt G. Do you want to stop with us?
Pompey. Yes, massa. I spec's I does.
Capt G. What's your name?
Pompey. Pompey Napoleon Washington Jackson.
Capt G. What can you do, Pompey?
Pompey. Can't do nuffin, massa.
Capt. G. Where did you come from?
Pompey. Come from down de road yere, a piece, I reckon on.
Capt G. Where do you live?
Pompey. Don't live nowhere, massa. Stops around anywhere I can get a place.
Capt. G. Are there many rebs over where you came from?
Pompey. Is dere many rebs? De wood is full of him. Dere is more than fourteen hundred thousand over yonder in dat tobacco field.
Capt G. Come into my quarters, and I will see if I can't find something for you to do.

They go into quarters. Captain gives him sword and piece of rag. POMPEY *comes out cleaning sword, takes off his coat and hat and throws them down side of tent, and comes down singing. Boys crowd around him.*

Bryant. Pompey, can you sing?
Pompey. No, massa; I never sing 'cept sometimes when I goes to meeting.
Bryant. Well, what do you sing there?
Pompey. We sings psalms, hymns, and odder tings.
Bryant. Give us one.
Pompey. Oh no! I can't, deed I can't; I never sings only to myself.
Bryant. Just once, Pompey, and we will join in the chorus.
Boys all say. Yes; give us a tune.
Pompey. Well, if you will join in the chorus, I will sing for you. (*Strikes up camp-meeting hymn. Boys join in the chorus.*)

Ord. Serg't II. (*Comes out of quarters.*) Boys, no dress parade this afternoon. (*Retires.*)

While the boys are singing chorus, FRITZ *is making violent gesticulations, as if in pain.*

Swift. Say, Billy, look at Fritz! See how pale he is.
Billy. What's the matter, Dutchy? Got the colic?
Fritz. I don't know what you call it, but I got sometings. I tink it was dat stuff vat the sturgeon gave me. I wish he got it back again!
Billy. Well, never mind. You will get over it soon. We will cure you. (BRYANT *takes* FRITZ *down front. They talk in dumb show. Boys bring in blanket.* BILLY *backs* FRITZ *into it. Boys toss him up.*)
Swift. How's that, Fritz? Don't that make you feel better?
Fritz. (*Speaking as he goes up and down.*) 'Tis all right when I go up, but ven I come down I don't like it. (*Bugle calls tattoo. Boys drop blanket and go into their tents.*)
Fritz. (*Shaking himself and muttering.*) I tink dat Billy makes himself a good doctor. I recommend him to cure the colic every time. If he got me mad I kick him all full of holes!

Serg't FOSTER *goes around to different tents with candles. Boys light up, come outside of tents, and sit down on stage smoking and talking in dumb show. Music and singing until taps. Taps beat, lights shut out, and all quiet. Long roll beat at a distance; taken up by drums in camp. Capt. G. comes out of tent and orders.*

Capt. G. Turn out, boys! Long roll! (*Men rush out in confusion.*)

BATTLE BUSINESS.   SCENE CLOSES.

SCENE II. — *Interior of the old Stone Church. Soldiers bringing in wounded men on stretchers. They bring in* ALPHONSE, *wounded in the leg.* BRYANT *follows behind the stretcher;* SWIFT *wounded in the head, supported by two soldiers.* FOSTER *wounded in the right shoulder, brought in by arms and legs. Two or three wounded Rebs brought in with others.* EDWARD, *wounded in left shoulder, brought in on stretcher,* HARRY *following.*

NURSES *and* SURGEON (MAUD *and* LUCY *as nurses*), *enter with the soldiers,* R. *and* L.

Harry. (*To* EDWARD.) There Ned, how do you feel now. Are you in much pain.
Edward. (*Speaking with effort.*) Not much Harry, don't mind me; go and look after some of the boys that are more badly wounded.

Reb. Priv. Small. Water; water; for the love of heaven give me just a drop of water.

Edward. Who is that calls for water? Harry, there is a little in my canteen; give it to the poor fellow. (HARRY *carries canteen to rebel private Small; gives him a drink.*)

Small. Thank you, Yank. You are a good fellow. Give us your hand. (*Shake hands.*) We are all on a level now, and we don't hold any hard feelings, do we?

Harry. No. Not one.

(LUCY *and other* NURSES *attend the wounded.*)

Maud. (*Goes to Swift.*) Where are you wounded?

Swift. In the head, marm. (*Rubbing his hand on wound.*)

Maud. (*Binding up his head.*) What company do you belong to?

Swift. Bay State Rifles, from Boston.

Maud. Bay State Rifles! Do you know Sergt. Huntington and Edward Clifford?

Swift. Yes, marm. Ned is badly wounded, and I think they brought him here, with the rest of us.

Maud. (*In coming down meets* HARRY. *In surprise each call the other by name.*) Are you wounded?

Harry. No. I escaped without a scratch, but how came you here?

Maud. I volunteered as a nurse, just after your company left home, and have been in Washington and following the army ever since. Is Edward here?

Harry. Yes, and very badly wounded.

Maud. Oh, where is he? take me to him.

Harry. (*Carries* MAUD *to where* EDWARD *is lying.*) Ned, here is some one you would like to see.

Edward. (*Opening his eyes in astonishment.*) Maud Huntington, am I dreaming?

Maud. No, dear Ned. It is I; thank heaven we meet again. Are you badly hurt?

Edward. I think not. I shall be all right by and by. But where did you come from?

Maud. From Washington. After you left I could not content myself with the listless, humdrum life at home, when I knew so many of our brave boys needed assistance. I came to Washington accompanied by Mrs. Clifton. We volunteered as nurses, and since then have followed the army, caring for the wounded and sick.

Edward. That's like you both, looking after the welfare of others, at the sacrifice of your own pleasure.

Maud. Edward, can you forgive me for thinking you were false? We called upon Mrs. Clifton as you requested, and heard from her lips the story of your kindness and charity.

Edward. I have nothing to forgive, Maud. My only regrets are that you could not have known the truth before.

Maud. And will you forget what has happened, and let us be to each other as we were before?

Edward. Aye. Gladly will I forget it; hereafter it shall never be mentioned between us, and if the thought of it ever comes to our minds it shall only bind us closer to each other, and make our love still stronger.

(ÉDWARD *grows faint.* MAUD *supports him.*)

(*Enter* PRIVATE HARRIS, *hurriedly.*)

Private Harris. The Rebs are coming down the road on the double quick. Those of you who can walk had better get out of this, if you don't want to be captured.

Alphonse. You had better go, Billy; there is no need of your staying to be taken.

Bryant. No, Phony, I promised your mother, when we left home, I would take care of you, and if I go and leave you I shan't be true to my word.

Alphonse. Never mind, Billy, go ahead; you are not wounded, and can easily get back to our lines.

Bryant. Well, if you say so, I will go; but I don't want to. I had rather stay, even at the risk of being taken prisoner.

(*Shakes hands with* PHONY, *and exit,* R.)

Edward. Harry, take Maud with you, and escape before it is too late.

Maud. No, Edward, I will stay with you, no matter what the risk.

Harry. That will be foolishness, Maud. If you were to stay you would only receive ill-treatment at the hands of these barbarians.

Edward. You must both go. It would be folly to stay.

Harry. Maud, fly with the surgeon, and these men who are not badly wounded. I am determined to stay with Ned, and you can't change my mind. Be quick. (MAUD *goes to* NED.) You haven't a minute to spare.

(MAUD *stoops down and kisses* NED, *then goes back to* LUCY.)

(*Enter* REBELS *headed by* MAJOR McKIE, COL. LOCKWOOD *with them, bringing in* BRYANT, *whom they have captured.*)

Lockwood. Major, pick out our men, send them to the rear and see that they are well cared for. These cursed Yankees you can put under guard; we will cart them to Richmond, they are so anxious to get there. (*Comes down to where* EDWARD *and* HARRY *are.*) (*Sarcastically.*) Holloa, who have we here? Gentlemen, this is indeed a surprise. I am delighted to see you, under the circumstances. Considering the very hospitable treatment I received from your father, my inclination would be to send you home; but my patriotism and duty to the cause I represent obliges me, very unwillingly I assure you, to send you to Richmond with the other prisoners. By the way, Mr. Clifford, how did you settle that little affair with your beloved? Did the old man take you back again? Are you married; or did Miss Maud think you too much married already?

Enter Rebel Cavalryman with despatches to MAJOR MCKIE, *during the above.* MAJOR MCKIE *comes down to* LOCKWOOD. MAUD *and* LUCY *also come down.*

Major McKie. (*Saluting.*) Colonel, information has been received from one of Capt. Toombs' spies that Col. Chas. Huntington will be the bearer of important despatches to Gen. Barry.

Lockwood. Have Capt. Toombs take his men down to the Stone Bridge. I will meet you there. (*Exit* MAJOR MCKIE, R.) (*To* HARRY.) If I am fortunate enough to capture your brother Charles, I assure you I shall not send him to Richmond. I will swing him up. He and I have a little private matter to settle. (*To* EDWARD.) I had almost forgotten. I have something belonging to you in my pocket. Oh, yes, here it is; the original letter you received from Lucy Clifton. (*Takes out letter, and holds it up.*)

Edward. Then you are the cause of all my misery. May heaven forgive you. I never can.

Harry. You are a heartless villain, Guy Lockwood, to taunt a poor wounded man in this way. You would not dare to do it if he did not lie here helpless.

Lockwood. Don't get excited, young man; keep cool. I hold no hard feelings against him. We were after the same object, your lovely sister. He wanted her for her love, and I for her money, and to all appearances neither of us will gain our object.

Edward. I will live in spite of all you can say or do, and will yet wed Maud Huntington.

Lockwood. (*Tauntingly shaking the letter in his face.*) Perhaps you will, young man; but you don't look much like it now, though.

(EDWARD *grabs letter and aims revolver at* LOCKWOOD. LOCKWOOD *draws sword, throws up* EDWARD's *arm.* LOCKWOOD *in the act of stabbing* EDWARD. LUCY *places cross in front of* EDWARD. *Tableau of Characters. Scene closes.*

SCENE III. — *A wood.*

Enter POMPEY, R.

Pompey. Dis is the worsted times I ever seed; tings aint now as they use to was. I'se just been down to see de ole woman, and such a mess as dere is down dere, I never seed. De ole woman is done gone off, and the whole roof is blown off de shanty. Nice and airy down dare now. Holloa, who's dis?

Enter MAUD *and* LUCY, R.

Maud. Oh, sir, can you direct us to the Union camp?

Pompey. Sartin sure I can, misses; you see dat ole shanty down dar, wid the roof clean gone. Well, you go down by dat, den you take the fust turn to de right; den you go along a piece till you come to the cross roads, and dat will bring you to de Union camp.

Lucy. Shall we be likely to meet any Rebels?

Pompey. Don't tink you will, misses; dey's done gone off the oder way. Aint seen any of the Johnnies anywhere around here for sometimes.

Maud. Heaven grant that we may be in time to warn brother Charles! It can't be more than two miles to camp, and if we can reach there in an hour we may save him. (*To* POMPEY.) Will you not go with us as far as the picket-lines?

Pompey. Ob course I will. I'se just going down dat way myself.   (*Exit* MAUD, LUCY *and* POMPEY, L.)

SCENE IV. — *Mountain Pass.*

CHARLES HUNTINGTON *comes down path, and enters on the stage from back,* L.

Charles. What a very lonely road this is to be on. I hope I haven't lost my way. I must proceed carefully, for I have yet three miles to go, and it won't do to be captured with these despatches on me. (*Examines revolver.*) Let me see. Pass the old mill and take the first right hand turn. (*Starts off,* L. U. E.) (*As he starts off, two Rebs come down from the right in rear of him. Rebs come in on each side of stage. Enter* COL. LOCKWOOD, MC-KIE *and* CAPT. TOOMBS, R. U. E.)

Col. Lockwood. Maj. McKie, search that man and see if you can find any important papers about him. (*Major searches* COL. HUNTINGTON; *takes papers and hands them to* LOCKWOOD.)

Lockwood. You didnt expect to see me here, did you? I have been waiting for you for the last hour, and began to think that I wasn't to have the pleasure of your company. Do you remember the last time we met? I promised you that if the fortunes of war permitted us to meet again, I should spare no pains to remind you how you blocked my little game. Well, here we are, and I hold the winning hand. What do you suppose I am going to do with you, eh Charles?

Charles. You can do nothing with me, according to the rules of civilized warfare, but keep me as a prisoner until I am exchanged.

Lockwood. Damn civilized warfare; what do you think I care for it. In your case I propose to take the law in my own hands. I am going to be judge, jury, and executioner. You see that tree over there? Well, I intend to try the strength of one of its limbs by suspending you by the neck from it. To come to the point, Charles, I am going to hang you if the cursed rope don't break.

Charles. You dare not do it. I am a commissioned officer in the Federal Army, and if you attempt to carry your barbarous threats into execution, my government will retaliate twofold.

Lockwood. Never mind that, I am willing to take the responsibility on my own shoulders. I'll do it first, and consider the results afterwards. String him up, you curs. (REBS *take* CHARLES *to tree, put rope around his neck and prepare to string him up.*)

Lockwood. What do you think now about my daring to hang you?

Maud. (*Appears suddenly back,* L.) I will tell you what he thinks, Guy Lockwood. You dare not hang him. (*As* MAUD *speaks, Rebel Soldier raises his musket to fire.* LOCKWOOD *starts up towards him, throws his gun up.*)

Lockwood. Put down your gun, fool. Leave her to me. (*To* MAUD.) Bravely said, sweet Maud. I admire your courage; but, it strikes me you are rather putting your head in the lion's mouth. (*Jestingly.*) On what terms shall we surrender?

Maud. Release my brother instantly, or I will fire.

Lockwood. Don't use such forcible arguments. I will tell you what I will do. If you will promise to marry me, I will agree to release your brother and send him back to camp. If you don't accept my proposition, I will swing him up, and take you along with me. What do you say? I will give you one minute to decide.

Maud. (*Waves handkerchief. Bugle sounds outside.*) There's my answer. (*Union troops come in and form tableau. Union soldier aims at* LOCKWOOD. *Soldier in act of cutting rope.* POMPEY *stands over. Characters range themselves.*)

MUSIC — *Yankee Doodle.*

TABLEAU.

ACT IV.

SCENE I. — *Rebel Stockade.* — *One year is supposed to have elapsed between third and fourth Acts.* — *Slow music.* — *Act opens with thunder-storm.* — *Characters arranged in different positions, lying down, walking, etc.* — HARRY *lying down back.* — *Rude shelter-tents of blankets, etc.*

Alphonse. Ain't it most time for them to serve out rations, Billy? I am so hungry.

Billy. I am afraid we shan't have anything to-day, Phony; our rations have been stopped for two days, so they say, because some of the boys were caught tunneling out.

Alphonse. It don't seem possible I can go without food much longer. O, Billy, I fear I shall never live to go home again.

Billy. Don't get down-hearted, Phony. Try and keep up a little while longer. We may be exchanged.

Harry. (*Coming down.*) Have any of you seen Ned this morning?

Swift. He has gone to take a walk over to the other side of the stockade.

Enter SERGEANT FOSTER, L.

Harry. Did you find out what the firing was about, last night?

Foster. Yes. They caught some of the men trying to escape, and fired on them. About fifty have got away, and they are after them now with the dogs. There is some talk about an exchange, but I don't know as it is true.

Harry. We have heard that story so many times before that I shan't believe it until I see it done. Oh, I wish it could be so, for I am dreadful tired of this life. (*Enter* EDWARD *with small bundle of wood,* R.) Why, Ned, where did you get that wood, and where have you been?

Edward. I helped to carry poor Dick Rogers out. He died about two hours ago, and we have buried him. Poor fellow, with his last breath he implored me to give him food. But I had none for him. This is the first time, Harry, since we have been shut up in this terrible place, that I have seen the outside of the pen. Oh, I cannot find words to describe how beautiful the grass and woods seemed to me. If what the Surgeon told me is true, there is some hopes that our sufferings will soon end.

Harry. What did he say, Ned?

Foster. Do you think there are any prospects of going home?

Edward. He said there would be an exchange shortly. But

we cannot place any confidence in what they say, for they have promised to do so before. (*Turns to* BRYANT.) How is Phony this morning, Billy?

Bryant. I think he is worse, Ned. I am afraid he is giving up altogether.

EDWARD, HARRY *and* BILLY, *go down to* PHONY.

Edward. Come, cheer up, Phony; don't give up in that way.

Alphonse. No, Ned, I cannot cheer up any more. In a little while I shan't want anything to eat, for I feel all gone here.

(*With great effort puts hand on stomach.*)

Billy. Don't talk so, Phony. I can't bear to hear you. Why, Phony, where's your ring?

Alphonse. (*Raising himself slowly.* BILLY *supports him.*) When I was out there (*pointing to right*), just now, an angel came and took it and gave it to my mother. (*Falls back dead.*)

TABLEAU. — *An Angel handing ring to* WIDOW DE PEYSTER. — *Slow music to end of tableau.*

Billy. Ah, Harry, he is dead. (*Characters come and look at him, murmur on stage, and resume their former positions.*)

Foster. Here comes McKie, boys.

Enter MAJOR McKIE *and two rebel soldiers.* R. *He goes around stage till he comes to* PHONY.

McKie. Halloa, boys, there's another ration less. Take off that carcass with the rest. Here, some of you Yanks, help lug it out.

Bryant. Please, Major, let me help bury him. He and I were friends.

McKie. No, stay where you are. If you go out there the dogs will bite you. (*Two soldiers take body out,* L.) Come, Sergeant, fall in your Yankee horde.

Foster. Come, fall in, boys. (*Men all fall in line.*)

(McKIE, *Reb soldier and* FOSTER *go down the line.*)

McKie. Don't see but you are all in good condition this morning; only one man from this squad gone to the Devil. (*Turns to* HARRY.) Ain't you got about sick of this? Come, go outside to work and get gray clothes, and plenty to eat.

Harry. No. I enlisted to serve my country, and I will never desert the cause.

McKie. (*To* EDWARD.) Won't you take the oath, or will you stay here and die of hunger?

Edward. You can starve my body, but you cannot stain my soul with treason.

McKie. Humph! (*To the other prisoners.*) Men are wanted to work down on the Islands, under guard, as prisoners. You won't have to take a musket. You are not obliged to go; but those who do go, will be made to perform the work required of them, whether they like it or not. In return, we will give you rations of flour, meat, rum and tobacco. All those who will avail themselves of this opportunity, can pick up their traps and get ready to leave the prison.　　　　(*Exit* McKie, R.)

(*Men start to follow him.*)

Edward. Stop! Fellow-prisoners. You have heard what this man has said. The work required of you is to dig rifle-pits for the enemy, though he has not squarely said so. You are called upon to desert the old flag, and to give assistance to our foe. Although many of you are slowly dying of hunger, yet it is treason to accept the proposition. I, too, am starving. You can see written all over me, long imprisonment. We are famishing; but let us show our enemies that we are not hirelings, but patriots; that we can die, but will not be dishonored. Is there one here, after suffering for so glorious a cause, that will brand himself with traitor?

(*Prisoners shout — No, No, Never! Prisoners sing chorus of Star Spangled Banner. Rebs outside sing chorus of Bonnie Blue Flag. Gun heard outside. Characters rush toward wing,* L. *Bryant goes out. Returns,* L.)

Foster. What was it, Billy?

Bryant. Nothing but a poor fellow who went over the deadline, and was shot.

Harry. He at least is out of misery.

(*Enter* COL. LOCKWOOD, McKIE *and Rebel Soldiers,* R.)

McKie. (*To* FOSTER.) Fall in your squad again, Sergeant. Tell your men to pack up their spare clothes, and pick up their traps. Some of you will have a chance to get out of this.

(*Men cry "Exchange!" "Exchange!" and fall in.*)

Lockwood. Pick out only such men, Major, as will never be able to enter the service again. My orders are, to exchange no man that can handle a musket again.

(MAJOR *goes down line and picks out* HARRY, EDWARD, FOSTER, BRYANT, *and others; these go to left.*)

McKie. Colonel, I have selected from this squad, if you will look them over, I will go to the other squad and pick out the men from them.　　　　(*Exit* McKIE *and Rebel soldiers,* L.)

Lockwood. (*Goes to squad selected men, looks them over until he comes to* HARRY *and* EDWARD.) What, you here! It seems as though we were fated to meet under all circumstances. So you have been picked out to be exchanged! (*To* HARRY.) Well, I guess you can go. As for you (*to* EDWARD), I guess you can stand it to stay a little while longer. You look hale and hearty.

Harry. Oh, please, Colonel, let him go with us! The Major picked him out.

Lockwood. We can't spare him; the officers here have become so attached to him that they cannot bear to give him up; besides, I have not forgotten, that in spite of me, he was going to marry your sister. But it won't be on this exchange. (*Jerks* EDWARD *to other side.*) Get over there with the rest of the scum. (HARRY *starts to go to* NED.) Where are you going?

Harry. If he must stay here, I am going to stay with him.

Lockwood. What disinterested friendship! You stay where you are, if you know when you are well off. (*Draws revolver. To reb soldier.*) March these men out to the gate.)

(*Men march out,* R. HARRY *gets out of ranks, and mixes with remaining prisoners. Comes down to* EDWARD *as he is fainting.*)

Edward. (*To* LOCKWOOD.) Oh, let me go with them! I am dying from hunger! Have you no heart, that you can see me here in this condition, and yet taunt me in such a manner? Here at your feet I humbly implore you to take me with you.

Lockwood. No; stay here and die like a dog. You shall never pass the threshold of that gate alive, if I can help it.

(*Exit,* R.)

Harry. Ned, don't give up. I will stay with you, and if we must die, we will starve together.

Edward. O Harry, why didn't you go when you had the chance?

Harry. Because I couldn't go and leave you here alone. Remember our tunnel, Ned; in that there is still a hope.

(PRISONERS *heard in the distance singing,* — "*We are going home.*")

CHARACTERS FORM TABLEAU.

SCENE II. — *Wood.* — *Exchanged prisoners march across stage, singing,* — "*We are going home.*"

SCENE III. — *Deep wood, trees at back.*

Enter HARRY, *with branch of tree, supporting* EDWARD, L.

Edward. I can go no further, Harry. I am completely worn out. My limbs refuse to support me.

Harry. Keep up a few moments longer, Ned. We can't be but a little way behind the other men. Hark! I hear some one coming. (*They retire back behind a tree,* L.)

Enter rebel PRIVATE SMALL.

Small. I thought I saw them pass this way. (*Rests his musket on stage ; looks off,* R.)

Harry. (*Creeping down behind him.*) Oh, if I can only have the strength to strike a decisive blow! (*Hits rebel. Rebel falls.* HARRY *drags reb out,* R., *taking his musket.*)

(*Enter* LOCKWOOD, L. *Sees* EDWARD. *Grabs him by the throat, drags him down front, and throws him upon the stage.*)

Lockwood. Now, then, I have got you. You thought to escape me, did you? If it had been any one else but you, I should not have taken the trouble to follow. I'll soon put an end to your miserable existence. (*Draws, and cocks his revolver.*)

Harry. Entering, R. I'll first put an end to yours. (HARRY *fires.* LOCKWOOD *drops the revolver, and falls.*)

Lockwood. You have done it for me this time, Harry Huntington! Oh, I could have met death upon the battle-field, and welcomed it; but to die here by your cursed hands! Ha! Ha! Don't think I am afraid of death! You cannot get away. Here Toombs, McKie, this way. (*Falls back dead.*)

TABLEAU BY CHARACTERS.

SCENE IV. — *Wood near the Coast.*

Enter JACK TARBOX *and* TOM MARLINSPIKE, L.

Tarbox. Well, shiver my timbers, but this are a queer place, Tom.

Tom. So it are, Jack. I reckon we must have lost our way. Let's go down 'ere a piece and take a hobservation.

Jack. All right, 'eave a'ead. I'll follow in your wake. We 'aven't got much more time to find the gig before dark.

Tom. No more we hain't, Jack. We had better be getting h'out of this 'ere blasted place. I don't like the looks of it. I should 'ate to fall into the 'ands of the henemy.

Jack. Right you are, Tom. But what are this a bearing down on us?

Tom. What, that 'ere h'object? Why, that's a h'african.

Jack. A h'african! What's a h'african?

Tom. Why, a hunbleached hamerican.

Enter POMPEY, *slyly,* R.

Jack. Come here, Nig. Where are we?

Pompey. 'Specs your here, ain't you?

Tom. Where's 'ere?

Pompey. In de woods, ob course. Is you blind?

Jack. Well, we want to go to the coast.

Pompey. Why de debil don't you go dar, den?

Jack. Can you show us the way?

Pompey. In course I can. What you doing out here? Dos you know where you are? Dere's Rebs all through dese woods.

Tom. Let's get h'out then. Nig, which way shall we go?

Pompey. Whar do you belong?

Jack. To the transport "Pembroke," bound for Fortress Munroe, with exchanged prisoners.

Pompey. Goin' norf, is you? Will you take me wid you?

Jack. Yes; you can go if you will help us out of here.

Pompey. Come along, den. I show you de way.

(*Business. Exit* POMPEY, *followed by* JACK *and* TOM, R.)

SCENE V. — *Deck of the Transport "Pembroke."* — CAPT. PERRY, LIEUT. HARRISON, *and Sailors discovered.* — *Sailors busy about decks.* — CAPT. PERRY *looking through spy-glass.*

Perry. Here they come, Mr. Harrison. I can see them, just down by the bend in the river. Send the boats ashore.

Harrison. Ay, ay, sir. (*Goes to side of vessel.*) All right there; shove off.

(*Cheers heard in the distance.*)

Perry. (*To* HARRISON.) Poor fellows; who can describe their sufferings? And how happy they must feel, to know that they will soon be under the protection of the old flag.

Harrison. It must, indeed, be a beautiful sight for them to behold, after their long imprisonment, — the stars and stripes again.

(*Cheers nearer.*)

Perry. Ay, and they appreciate it, too. This will be the fifth load of exchanged prisoners I have carried home; and the scenes that I have witnessed on the deck of this vessel have been heart-rending, and impossible to describe. Men, both old and young, and of all classes, so famished and weak that they could hardly crawl, have got up here on the quarter-deck, and sat for hours watching that flag, the tears streaming down their cheeks, and the only words coming from their lips, " Thank God! Thank God! "

(*Loud cheering outside.*)

Harrison. Here they are now. Bear a hand there. (SAILORS *go to side, and assist* PRISONERS *on deck.*—BILLY BRYANT. SWIFT, FOSTER, *and others.* — SWIFT *sits down by the side of the vessel, looks up at the flag, and commences to cry.*)

Billy. What's the matter, Swift? What are you crying about?

Swift. (*Pointing to flag.*) I can't help it, Billy; I feel so happy.

Billy. (*Turns away, almost crying.*) Well, there's no use crying about it.

Foster. (*Goes to* CAPT. PERRY.) Captain, couldn't you haul that flag down a little —just so we can touch it, only to see if it's real?

Perry. Certainly, if it will be any satisfaction to you. I will do so in just one moment. (*Going to* LIEUT. HARRISON.) Everything is in readiness. Give orders to get underweigh.

Harrison. But, sir, Jack Tarbox and Tom Marlinspike are ashore in the gig.

Perry. Send a boat ashore after them.

Harrison. All right, sir. (*Goes to give orders.*)

Perry. (*Taking his glass and looking.*) Wait a moment, Mr. Harrison. I see them now. No, it ain't them; it appears like two prisoners. They are running along the shore, and making motions to us. What is that behind them? Heaven have mercy on them, it is two blood-hounds, coming down the hill, in full chase! They cannot escape! Ah, good! there's a boat coming out of the creek, just in front of them. It's Jack and Tom in the gig. The prisoners see them! They wade out into the water! Now they are taken into the boat! (*Characters all cheer.*) Just in time; not a second to spare! Thank heaven, they are saved! (*Shot fired outside.*) Good, Tom; that bloodhound will never track another Union man.   (*Pause.*)

Here they are! (*Cheers. Men all go to side of vessel. As* HARRY *and* NED *enter,* CAPTAIN *hauls down flag.*)

Enter HARRY, *supported by* TOM, *and* NED, *by* POMPEY *and* JACK

Harry. See, Ned, the old flag! Safe, safe, at last!

(MUSIC. — "*Star-Spangled Banner.*")

TABLEAU BY CHARACTERS.

ACT V.

SCENE I. — *Room in Huntington's house. — Characters discov-ered. — Slow music. — Slow Curtain.*

Huntington. (*To* DOCTOR.) How do you think he is this morning, Doctor?

Dr. Swett. (*Shaking his head.*) I see no change, either for better or worse. In a few moments the fever will have reached its crisis, and we shall then know whether he will live or die.

Maud. Will he not recover consciousness again, Doctor? For two weeks he has been delirious, and has recognized no one. Is there no hope?

Dr. Swett. While there is life, there is hope.

Harry. Few could have gone through what he has and lived to reach their home; for besides the hardships he has undergone, he was suffering from his wound. Many a man, but for his cheering words of comfort, would have laid himself down in despair to die.

(EDWARD, *delirious, opens his eyes wildly, tries to raise himself up.*)

Edward. Follow me, boys! I'll lead you on! Rally around the flag, and every man stand firm! Ha! Ha! Guy Lockwood, you wrote that letter! You are the man who has caused me so much misery! But I will live in spite of you!—Oh, please let me go with the other men. I am so hungry. I am starving here. Oh, let me go! Hark, Harry, do you hear the blood-hounds! See! they are after us! Let's get into the brook, and then they cannot track us! — That's it! That's it! Now up that tree! — There's a Union vessel! Do you see the old flag flying there? Isn't it glorious!—Harry, the hounds are after us again! Quick into the boat! There, now we are safe! (*Falls back exhausted.*)

Lucy. (*Goes to* MAUD.) O Maud, this is terrible.

(EDWARD *again opens his eyes.*)

Edward. Where am I? (*Pause.*)

Dr. Swett. The crisis has passed — he will live.

Maud. Thank heaven. (*Comes around to front of cot and kneels down.*) Do you know me, Edward?

Edward. Yes; it is Maud. (*She takes his hand.*) Is Harry here?

Harry. Here I am, Ned. (*Assisted to* NED.)

Huntington. Edward, you have been very sick; very near to death's door; but thanks to the mercy of the Infinite Father, you are now out of danger. Rest easy here, for you are in my house, and shall be cared for as my son. Your every wish shall be anticipated, and all that can be done, shall be done for you.

Dr. Swett. He must be kept very quiet, and avoid all excitement. A relapse at this time would prove fatal.

Maud. He shall receive the best of care, Doctor, be assured of that. We love him too well not to do all we can to aid his recovery. Beside his being very dear to us as a friend, we owe him a debt of gratitude that we can never repay. He has served his country faithfully; has fought nobly in her defence; and all that we might live at home in peace, and that the Union might be maintained.

Edward. For all the sufferings I have endured I am amply repaid in knowing I have done my duty. And now the prospects are that our nation will be triumphant in this glorious struggle, I am proud that my name will forever go down to posterity as one of our country's defenders.

TABLEAU. — OUR COUNTRY'S DEFENDERS.

END OF DRAMA.

www.ingramcontent.com/pod-product-compliance
Lightning Source LLC
Chambersburg PA
CBHW030903260626
47169CB00008B/2655